The Adorable

Duke

Audrey Manor Series

Book One

Marie Leick

ISBN: 9798851579868
Imprint: Independently published

The story, all names, characters, and incidents portrayed in this production are fictitious. No identification with actual persons (living or deceased), places, buildings, and products is intended or should be inferred.

Book Cover by GetCovers.com

First edition 2023

The Adorable Duke

The Adorable Duke

Prologue

Lulworth Abbey, Dorset – 1804

> *"Amazing grace how sweet the sound*
> *That saved a wretch like me*
> *I once was lost, but now I'm found*
> *Was blind but now I see."*

Franny was singing as she worked in the gardens of Lulworth Abbey. At sixteen years of age, she had been living under the care of the monks and nuns at the abbey since she was eight. As her beauty and age increased, the monks grew evermore nervous when they walked near her. The few nuns that lived at the abbey realized they needed to move Franny elsewhere and prepared her for a future role of governess by educating Franny with a wealth of knowledge across many subjects, under the strictness of the nuns' discipline. The plan was for her to stay until she turned eighteen for that was when the secretive funds that supported Franny, and most of the abbey, would cease. All that changed on the day she was singing in the garden attending to the medicinal herbs.

"Miss Lane! Miss Lane, come here posthaste," called out Sister Mary Marguerite. Franny glanced up to see Sister Mary with a rather tall, older man dressed as a gentleman.

Oh no, the day has come. I am to be married to an old man. Perhaps he needs a wife to attend his children or hopefully just a governess. I hope it is as a governess. Surely, the sisters would not dare sell me to be a concubine. Would they?

Nervously, Franny cleaned her hands with the drab, cream apron she wore over the drab, brown dress. She approached the stranger and Sister Mary. Giving a curtsy and keeping her head down, she spoke in a soft, sweet voice, "Good day, sir. Good tidings, to you Sister Mary."

The gentleman took his hand and gently raised her head examining her eyes. "My child, my daughter, I have finally found you. By God, you look so much like your beautiful mother." Lord Nathaniel Richard Lane, the 7th Duke of Millington, was awestruck in the presence of Franny. Tears filled his eyes as he fell to his knees. At last, after four years of searching, he finally found the daughter produced from his first and only love.

When Franny peered into his eyes, she knew it was her father. Their eyes were the same, a mix of browns and greens that changed with the light and brightness of the sun. In shock, she turned to Sister Mary and questioned, "Father?"

"Yes child, this is your father. Today, your life will change," responded Sister Mary.

And changed it did – most indeed.

Chapter One

Audrey Manor, Kent – February 1815

"**B**lake, my good man there you are. Thank you for having Mouse ready." Miss Francesca Maria Lane, otherwise known as Franny, stood tall at five feet and ten inches. Her long legs and arms toned from the years of riding her trusted thoroughbred named Mouse. Franny's body was what happened when athleticism mixed with refinement – curvy, lean, elegant, and beautiful all at once. Blake, the stable master, always depicted the perfect, tasty temptation. His shorter stature did not hinder his attractiveness. It was hard to resist staring at his triangled torso and sweet buttocks. Franny can only imagine the corded muscle definition and washboard abdomen beneath the tight fitted, white shirt. All the lifting and work as a groomsman sculpted his dignified shoulders and powerful neck. He rolled his shirt sleeves to just above the elbows, highlighting the fortitude of his robust forearms. The man looked simply delicious.

Blake constantly stirred Franny's imagination. He was the man that entered her dreams at night, causing her to do promiscuous acts upon her sex. Blake was the figure who appeared in her mind while she closed her eyes and took matters into her own hand when seeking release. It was his image that appeared while she was in the bath, wishing her finger were his tongue that produced the climatic sensation to her clit.

Franny learned how to pleasure herself one night at the abbey in Dorset, where she spent most of her childhood, when she spied on Sister Mary Marguerite. Franny was under the care and guidance of the sisters at the covenant she was banished to. Sister Mary was younger than the rest of nuns and kinder to Franny. One night, Franny heard faint whimpers from Sister Mary's room, so she peeked through the door's keyhole to see if anything was amiss. Franny witnessed the bliss that Sister Mary originated upon herself by using her hands – one hand upon her quim and another teasing the puckered nipple atop her breast. That same night Franny discovered for herself what Sister Mary heeded. Even at the age of fourteen, Franny understood her chances of finding love and marriage were indeed very trifle. At least she would be able to please herself when the urge arose.

Franny didn't need help to mount her horse, but to just feel Blake's strong hands assisting her onto the saddle was a small thrill she treasured each time she went for a ride. His wife was a lucky woman, and apparently well pleased, as she just gave birth to their sixth child. Franny longed for a love match. A match built on respect, a partnership, and passion to last all eternity. A match she knew would never happen for a woman like her, but she had come to terms with that notion long ago. Now she relished her freedom as a spinster who was financially independent.

"I am going to ride out to inspect the new irrigation ditches. We are praying the project is complete before the spring rains. Shalt be but a mere few hours. Back before afternoon tea." Blake held his bare hand to assist Franny to saddle Mouse. Purposely, Franny waited to put her riding gloves on until she was on top of the horse. She looked forward to Blake's callous hand brushing the inside of her palm, producing shivers throughout her being.

Blake never gave Franny a second glance. He was too in love with his wife. This actually made Franny more at ease in his presence since most men admired her with eyes of a predator - ready to pounce on fresh meat. Franny was half-Italian, considered by the *ton* as an exotic. Her light olive skin, along with her long, silky, thick black hair, and eye color that rumored to change with her moods, created a mysterious aura. To the *ton* of London Society, an exotic woman was only good for bedding, not wedding. At seven and twenty, the slight brush of skin-to-skin with the scrumptious groomsman was all Franny experienced regarding the sensation of a man's touch. She was past the considerate age for being on display at the marriage mart.

For the past eleven years, there was no time, no opportunity for Franny to enjoy a coming out ball or the London season. She had to raise two younger brothers, with the oldest being the Duke of Millington. Besides, the *ton* only spread dreadful rumors of her and would never fully accept her as one of them. A future of having her own family and household to oversee would never happen. Franny dedicated all her efforts to the success of her brothers and the family's estates. Through her work and the caretaking of her siblings, she found happiness, peace, and a place of belonging. Something she once thought was only a dream.

On the way to inspect the irrigation project, Franny lead Mouse into a hard-pressed gallop. Disregarding any propriety, she took off her riding hat and unpinned the back of her hair. The wind blowing through the strands of her hair made her feel free. Tears started to trickle down her face, not from emotion, at least she didn't think so, but rather from the crisp early spring air. Bringing Mouse into a canter, Franny took a few deep cleansing breaths. She closed her eyes.

Inhale.

Exhale.

The scents of evergreen, along with a salt air that drifted inland with the coastal wind filled her. Relaxation flowed down her body from her head to the tips of her toes.

Peace.

The vast coastal lands of her family's country estate, the envy of the upper echelon, claimed a quarter of Kent and rested between

Dover and Ramsgate. She opened her eyes and that was when she noticed him. A man, unknown to her, was fishing on the family grounds. Not just any strange man but one that was lean, muscular, and impeccably dressed. His body was that of a god – solid as a rock. She started to hold a conversation with her horse and spoke, "He must be well-bred and high-born, but why is he fishing in my favorite spot?" Franny directed the stallion to trot closer to the trespasser.

Who was the dashing stranger? He stood and turned, facing her direction. Tall, so very tall. At least six feet and four, maybe five inches. Handsome, so insanely handsome. Dark brown hair with lighter highlights and his body was strong. So strong. No padding necessary. With his clawhammer coat off, he was in a white shirt with no neckcloth, a black vest and wearing buckskin breeches with black riding boots. *Why does he have to have his shirtsleeves rolled to just below the elbows?* Franny thought, *"I am a sucker for bared forearms."* Some kind of force drew her closer, dangerously closer.

"I've never seen a more beautiful and mysterious creature in all my days," Lord Bennett David Wheeler, the 6th Duke of Kentwood, quietly declared to himself.

He was staring at a goddess. She was on top of a very tall black and brown stallion, at least sixteen, perhaps seventeen hands. Her black hair was flowing in the wind, and she wore a majestic purple riding habit. The fabric settling perfectly on the stunning thoroughbred, draped the horse like a royal robe, casting an illusion of total authority. *Was she riding astride?* Kentwood pictured her strong legs wrapped around him. The scene was a masterpiece come to life and it was riding right towards him. Kentwood realized he was a bit chubbier in a particular region of his breeches and failed to breathe. "What the bloody hell? Oh, bugger," he grumbled.

No woman before had aroused Kentwood like this. The dominatrix of a woman had awakened his Little Buddy, who tended to have a want and mind of his own. In times like these, Kentwood tried to think of things less attractive – like his governess with the huge mole on her cheek that had whiskers protruding from it. *There, that's better now. Hold it together, Bennett.*

Franny brought Mouse to a stop. The beast lifted his right front hoof and forcefully stomped the ground as if to say, *"Who the hell are you?"* Franny glared at Kentwood with fierce dark green eyes. She sat up straight in a possessive pose and spoke with a firm tone, "Good day sir. Pray tell as to why you are fishing at this particular pond? I daresay, you do not look familiar. Are you poaching? You do not appear as if you have no means of providing food for your family. These lands belong to the Duke of Millington." Her glare remained fixated on the attractive stranger awaiting his response.

Staring down the impressive man, Franny was almost overcome with the vapors. *Oh my, his eyes are filled with temptation.* Almond shaped, honey brown, gorgeous long lashes, and the tiniest mole perfectly placed at the side of his right eye. *So captivating and simply adorable. His children would be most beautiful. What is going on with me? Focus on the matter in front of you.*

"Excuse me?" Kentwood said in an irritated voice as he stood with his arms crossed in front of his chest. He was not used to such vulgarities and defiantly would not tolerate being talked down to as if he was a servant. *I am a duke for Christ's sake!* "Let me clarify just who I am. I am the Duke of Kentwood, and you will address me as Your Grace. I am a guest of the Duke of Millington and have permission to fish this pond," Kentwood said as he tried to assert his *highness* by talking in a stern ducal voice. He shook his head and continued, "Why am I explaining myself to you?"

Kentwood remedied that this common chit needed to be reminded of her place in society, and he was going to give her that very lesson – even if he was shaking in his boots just a little. On top of her horse, she had the command of Artemis. Yet, all he could think of was how beautiful she looked. He wished he were that very horseflesh, and she was straddling him. Kentwood protested, "What is wrong with me?"

"I'm sorry, what did you say?" Franny snapped back. She was very perturbed by the inflection of Kentwood's voice and mannerisms.

Bollocks, she has excellent hearing. "I said that I am a guest of the Duke of Millington who owns this pond and the lands *you* are trespassing on. Therefore, *you* should move on, my lady." *Did her eyes just turn from green to a shade of brown?* The faster this chit was out of his sight, the better. Her immense beauty unhinged everything inside of Kentwood. He was instantly mesmerized by her. Perhaps besotted, but that was not possible since Kentwood strongly believed a person does not instantly fall in love at first sight.

Franny slightly squinted her eyes, gave a little huff of disgust, and said, "First, you are the rudest, most conceited arse of a man I have ever been in the presence of. Second, I am not a lady." She then turned her mount towards the irrigation project she needed to inspect and galloped off - all the while she sarcastically thought, *"Great, way to keep it together Franny. Nothing like impressing your brother's guest with your splendid and humorous wit and charm. And the fact that he is the most gorgeous man, well that's just the icing on the cake."*

Kentwood was dazed. He picked up his fishing gear as he watched Franny trod away. Never in his life had a woman captured his whole person or made Little Buddy immediately stand at attention the way she did. Talking to himself out loud, Kentwood went through a checklist:

"I am not drunk."

"I do not use any snuff."

"I didn't smoke anything."

"Did I just have a mishap of the brain?"

"I am going mad. That is all there is. I am mad," Kentwood told himself as he shook his head. He was in need of a good, strong drink to clear his thoughts.

"Your Grace, how was your tour of the grounds?" Lord Edward Nathaniel Lane, the young, 8th Duke of Millington, quickly nodded his head in recognition of Kentwood's return. Millington was just two and twenty and already acknowledged by the realm as an expert in ducal economy. He may be young to manage so many estates, thirteen total, but his poise was of the strength and confidence of a seasoned monarch. He walked with a fearless strut. A brut of a man, he was six feet and five inches and built like a solid oak tree. His chestnut hair and hazel eyes, mixed with both the sands of the Sahara and the seas of the English Channel, created a picture-perfect duke of stoic strength.

"Millington, you have done your ancestors proud. I can only hope that Bayberry will be as half as majestic once improvements are final." After inheriting the dukedom, it was made clear that Kentwood's father did not put one pence into the upkeep of Bayberry Hall, the estate that rested adjacent to Millington's Audrey Manor. Bayberry was where Kentwood spent most of his childhood and he vowed to make it great again.

"Thank you, Kentwood. That compliment is most welcome. I admire your determination to restore your family's country estate to its former glory." Millington continued the conversation, "Did you get a moment to enjoy some fishing?"

Kentwood was attempting to recover from his encounter with Franny, trying to wrap his head, well both of his heads, around the enchantress that shocked his system. Keeping his inner thoughts to himself, he made sure his outside image reflected a snobby elitest and said, "I'm afraid the fishing was interrupted by a common chit with no propriety or respect for those above her." Just as Kentwood said those words, he spotted the very woman riding towards Millington and him. "Speak of the Devil and all his hellfire, here comes the humdrum, twit of a woman now."

Millington turned around to see his beloved sister. With a sound of disgust and warning, Millington grounded his teeth and declared to Kentwood, "That is Miss Francesca Lane. My sister, Your Grace."

Stunned and embarrassed, Kentwood stepped beside Millington, shoulder to shoulder, to make further observations. The pair of dukes made for a fine picture for all the virginal debutants and their meddling mothers who wished for a bite at a prestigious title. For a moment, the older Kentwood was physically intimated by Millington. He was used to being the tallest and strongest in the room, but Millington would edge him out in a battle of fists.

Looking from Millington to Franny, Kentwood noticed that tallness ran in the family. She was tall for a woman - just shy of six feet he would guess. Kentwood thought, "*What is with this family and their height? I wonder what it would be like in bed with a tall woman. I think the tallest I've woman I have enjoyed was five feet and four inches. What am I thinking? Just stop this madness. Her very brother is about to pound you because of your insulting remarks. I should just be myself and not try to be the arse that everyone expects me to be.*" He noted

The Adorable Duke

that Franny's skin tone was several shades darker than Millington, as if she bathed in the warmth of the Mediterranean sun. Something was amiss here. Kentwood had to find out. "I did not know you had a sister."

"Yes, Your Grace, she is older than I," answered a perturbed Millington. His hands formed to make fists as he crossed his arms in front of his chest, taking a very defensive stance. He braced for the comments Kentwood would say next. It never failed how the nosy, gossipmongers of the *ton* made the most absurd elaborate assumptions. Kentwood inquired, "I see. Your father's by-blow, I presume."

The words Kentwood used to describe Franny made Millington's blood boil and he could feel his ears increasing in heat. Scrunching his face in disconcert, Millington briefly lost control of his emotions, turned to Kentwood, and looked slightly down on him but still square in the eye, and with a lowered voice that rumbled a stern warning, "Your Grace, with all due respect, never, ever refer to my sister with that term or any term that is related again. I do not give a damn about who you are or the length of your peerage. I will lay you out."

Kentwood started to chuckle. The contemplation Millington was giving him was the same look Miss Lane gave him at the fishing pond.

"Perhaps, Kentwood, you find what I said comical or in jest, but if you continue to laugh at my family's expense, I will not hesitate

18

to break your perfectly formed nose," Millington said, reinforcing his disgust of Kentwood's comments regarding Franny.

Still laughing, Kentwood apologized and slapped Millington on the back. "Easy young pup. Easy. Forgive me. You and your sister have the exact same expression when perplexed. I couldn't help but chuckle at the strong resemblance between the two of you when you berated me like a child just now. She gave me the identical dressing down at the fishing pond. Seriously, it is a remarkable kinship you have. I'm actually relieved she is recognized by the family." Trying to change subject of the rising volatile conversation, Kentwood redirected, "Speaking of peerage, how is it that your ducal line is on its eighth duke but yet my line is older, and I am only the sixth?"

Millington looked at Kentwood as if he would love to punch him in the face and coldly stated, "We like to kill people who insult our family, and it sometimes leads to a younger death."

"Noted," responded Kentwood with a surprised, self-concerned face.

"My sister is recognized and much beloved. I would lay down my life for her. She has sacrificed so much for me and my brother. There is no finer lady that graces this great Earth. Here she approaches. I will make a formal introduction and you can see for yourself that she is not a common chit as you dictated." Millington's persona warmed with the oncoming approach of Franny.

Franny brought Mouse to a stop and dismounted without assistance. The riding habit slightly rose up her legs and revealed white stockings that went to just above the knees. Kentwood raised a brow as he noted Franny's toned, long legs - elegance and temptation combined. *Perfection.* Kentwood smiled slightly, realizing that she indeed was riding astride, and he needed to calm his Little Buddy again. All he could picture were her legs wrapped around his body as he rode her to ecstasy. *What is bloody wrong with me? Think of your first tutor - the one with yellow teeth that wouldn't stop smiling, displaying that one front tooth that hung lower than the rest.* Little Buddy was calm once again.

Franny noticed Kentwood's grin. *Oh, dear Lord above, those perfectly lined, white teeth and is that a dimple? Simply charming. Surely, he will take over my dreams this evening. How can I be so attracted to this arrogant cad?* Taking off her riding gloves and walking to them, Franny started the greeting, "Edward, darling, how was your meeting with the contractor this morning?" She ignored Kentwood's presence and kissed Millington once on each cheek.

Millington responded, "The meeting went splendidly. Repairs to the mill will be completed on time. How is the irrigation project coming along?"

Franny proudly lifted her head, glared at Kentwood, and rolled her eyes turning back to Millington with a smile and answered, "I am happy to report the project appears finished, despite all the cold and snow we have suffered this winter. Now we wait for the next rain to see if it will suffice."

Kentwood noted that her eyes were hazel. *Captivating.*

Realizing he forgot about introductions, Millington turned to Kentwood and said, "Forgive me, Your Grace, this is my sister, Miss Francesca Lane. Sister, this is Lord Bennett Wheeler, the Duke of Kentwood."

Kentwood dipped his head in a bow and grabbed Franny's bare hand with his. He placed his lips just close enough to her skin so she could feel his air hoover above her palm. "My lady, it is nice to make your *formal* acquaintance. Francesca is a beautiful name. Italian? No? Do you happen to go by Franny?"

His touch sent Franny's heart racing. Her chest was heaving, and an ache started to build deep within her mons. He had the hands of a man who spent his life working the lands and chopping wood – even Blake's touch didn't unhinge Franny this way. And those dimples! She needed to get control for at any moment she most certainly would swoon. Reminding herself that she could in no way possible, even remotely hold Kentwood in high regard, she peered at him with frustrated, squinted eyes and with the voice of an annoyed governess who was tired of misbehaving children said, "Did you say Kentwood? As is the neighboring dilapidated estate, Bayberry? If that is the case, my name is *Miss Lane*. And to remind you once again, I am not a lady, and you shall never be allowed to call me Franny."

Looking back and forth between Kentwood and Franny, Millington was curiously dumbfounded at the tension between the two. Ever the peacemaker, he recovered the introduction debacle from Franny's comments. "Ah, well... sister, the Duke of Kentwood will be our guest for the next month while repairs are underway at his estate. He wished to stay close by to keep up with the progress."

"Yes, your brother is extremely kind with his generosity, and I thank him. I hope it will not disturb you… my presence around you that is." Kentwood couldn't help but make the verbal jab to Franny.

Millington interjects, "Francesca does not stay at the main house. She has taken residence at the dower house." Shaking his head he continued, "Not sure why I just announced that." With eyes a bit wider and speaking with his mouth slightly opened but teeth clamped down, Millington asked Franny, "Will you dine with us this evening and privilege us with a concert, *dearest sister*?"

Responding in the same demeanor, Franny said, "Yes, *darling brother*. I will be present at seven. Until then, I bid you both a good day." And with that statement, Franny turned and never looked back.

Both gentlemen watched as Franny took her leave.

Arms folded across his chest, a smile on his face, with his head shaking side-to-side, Millington asked, "What did you do to my sister?"

Kentwood dropped his chin and sighed, "Millington, I know you gave a warning about my viewpoint of your sister. However, my ducal assessment of her character is unchanged. Pray, forgive me."

Millington said in a teasing voice, "No Kentwood, pray forgive me, but I think you and my sister are completely and ridiculously besotted. Two very stubborn besotted people."

"Don't be ridiculous! Besotted? *Pish posh*. How can one be *besotted* when the parties hardly know each other? Especially when first impressions were as low as possible," spoke a very annoyed Kentwood.

Millington, pat the back of Kentwood and let out a chuckle, "You best start swimming. You are drowning in besottedness."

Kentwood let out a low growl. "That's a ridiculous word, besotted. Why must you keep using it?"

"Because it annoys you, Your Grace," said Millington with a departing elbow jab to Kentwood's side.

Chapter Two

Franny approached the main house of Audrey Manor. An impressive sight, the house was built with various colors of gray and light brown stone with embedded exquisite, geometric patterns. The horseshoe shape had the east and west wings jetting out towards the front grounds, leaving the main entrance nested back. The elevated front entrance welcomed visitors with magnificent columns and stairs, highlighted with large oak doors ornamented with carvings depicting an ocean cliffside scene of tranquility, based on the White Cliffs of Dover. A true piece of art. The wings were surrounded with English Yew and remnants of pale pink roses that will soon flourish again with the approaching warming spring weather. The home was only two stories high, but the length was impossible to take in with one's eye. It boasted over one hundred twenty plus rooms and a cellar that would make any king green with envy.

Dressed in a deep-red colored gown with little flair and a plunging v-cut neckline that highlighted her bosom, Franny entered the library to treat herself to a pre-dinner drink and to find a good read for later that evening. She didn't need to wear exuberant jewelry or embellish her gowns. Franny's athletic body wore clothing like a glove fits a hand – tight, yet flowing, hugging every glorious curve of her body just so. She was proud of showing her tall, robust physique. It made her feel powerful amongst conceited high society. Along with her perfected repugnance glare and the fact that she was usually the tallest woman, sometimes person in the room, her presence oozed power. She poured a glass of wine and headed to the warmth of the fire. "Do you mind pouring a glass for me, Miss Lane?" He was there - Kentwood.

The Duke was dressed in a trimmed black velvet dinner jacket with silver buttons, a deep blue paisley vest, perfectly tied white ascot, and tight-fitting black trousers with boots. He looked like a Rouge of the First Water. Observing the library's collection of books, Kentwood folded his hands behind his back and approached Franny. He was bewitched by the beauty of her. Inside he was desperate to learn more about her - to touch her. Little Buddy wouldn't subside until he did. As soon as Kentwood came into Franny's presence, he had to think about his cook naked in the water closet to get Little Buddy under control. His cook, Mrs. Paddington, was a bubbly, older woman with many layers to her body, much like a flaky puffed crumpet - not one of Kentwood's typical bed-sport partners.

Franny dipped her head slightly and let out a small sigh and thought, *"This man is going to be a thorn in my side for a month!"* She poured the glass of wine and presented it to Kentwood. As he reached for the goblet, he allowed his fingers to linger for a moment upon hers. The touch sent fire through Franny's arm. She glared at him in disgust as if to give him a dressing down for his lack of manners. He looked down at her with eyes full of passion and a smirk that caused his lips to curve slightly higher on one side, showing off only one dimple.

Rake! Oh, my his is gorgeous. Franny needed to fan herself. She was temporarily paralyzed by her wanting to kiss the man. Instead of acting on the foolish impulse of wanton passion, Franny nervously blurted out, "Are you the one they call the Adorable Duke? The duke no one can take seriously because he is too pretty? The one all the mamas and debutantes are trying to trap just so they can have cute, adorable children?"

"Well, that is one way to ruin the mood," Kentwood thought. She was so very bold and direct. Kentwood growled and violently jerked his hand away with the wine glass, only to have some drink fall on his fingers. Shaking off the drops of alcohol, and licking off what lingered on his flesh, he downed the wine. Then proceeded to pour himself another round.

Franny was amused at her ability to fluster Kentwood and continued, *"Tsk, tsk.* With that reaction, I must conclude the topic of your *adorableness* is a touchy subject." Franny had the habit of putting more wood on a fire until it became out of control. "But truly, your children will be most charming, especially if they inherit those dimples." Franny drank her wine with a pinky extended and let out a little giggle to ascertain her small victory over Kentwood.

Instead of leaving the library, Kentwood decided to push his charm to the limit and set out to discover just how steadfast Miss Lane was in her verbal ridicule of his person. *Two can play this game.* With a villainous grin and luring eyes, he slowly came up to Franny and lowered his lips to her temple. At first the lemon and lavender scent of her hair overtook him, but he was no spring duckling. Skillfully, he said in a low, seductive growl, "You like my dimples, Miss Lane?"

Blast! He wasn't retreating. Without giving it a second thought, Franny turned her eyes at his and said, "No. They look cute on children, but not on a grown man. No less on a duke."

Wench. Taking the back of his hand and softly rubbing down the side of her cheek, Kentwood responded, "That's a shame. Most women dream of making babies with me and the *pleasure* I can give them."

What a bag of dicks! Franny's breathing accelerated. She was imploding. A pool of wetness besieged her womanhood. She remained poised. Eying at his neckcloth, she placed one of her hands on his chest and then slid her fingers to play with a button on his jacket. With a long blink she brought her eyes back up to him and said in the sultriest of voice, "Not all women." As she started her retreat, she allowed her finger to leave the button it was fascinated with and lightly linger down the edge of his jacket. She turned and left the room.

Damnation! Kentwood was flabbergasted at Miss Lane's actions. Little Buddy was most undeniably in love with her. *Oh fuck, not again.* This time Kentwood thought of Lord Crump, a pig of a man, eating his shepherd's pie with mouth fully opened and food flying out everywhere. *That's better. Now I can proceed to leave the room without a sword protruding outward from my midsection.*

Joining Kentwood, Millington, and Franny at the dinner table was Lord Miles, the youngest of the Lane siblings, but only a year younger than Millington. He was a smart, sweet lad who proficiently spoke three languages aside from his native tongue. Miles was tall and muscular as Millington but opposite in coloration. Millington resembled their father and Miles took after their mother – with sandy blonde hair and spellbinding hazel eyes of blue and green. He possessed charm and a sharp wit and a flirtatious personality that made the ladies swoon at his feet. Everyone loved Miles – the family's funny man and great negotiator.

Kentwood admired how the brothers and sister got along so splendidly. Franny was a wonder with her stories of keeping her two brothers in hand in the depths of their hellraising adolescent years. She was not the same woman that he encountered in the library just a brief while ago. This woman was filled with spirit and joy. Her laugh was a delight. "I must say that observing the three of you is very refreshing.

A family that enjoys their own company is a treasure. I admit, I am bit jealous," Kentwood confessed.

Miles asked, "Your Grace, are you an only child?"

"I had a brother. He was the heir, the anointed one in my father's eyes. Sadly, he died when we were young. My parents never recovered and hence here I am carrying on the ducal line." Kentwood gestured outward with his hands and lifted his glass to the rest of the table. "Enough of my sob story. A toast. I declare this dinner the great rebirth of a strong friendship between two powerful families, the Lanes and the Wheelers. May we continue our lineages and prosper together."

Everyone except Franny responded, "Here, here!"

Franny questioned, "Edward how is it that the Duke of Kentwood and you are acquainted?"

"Through the Earl of Warwick and his brood of sons," Millington responded.

"Ah yes, the Seven Sons of Warwick. Legendary. Thank you for the resolution, brother," Franny said as she sipped some wine.

With a mouth full of food, Miles chimed in, "Kentwood and Warwick's heir went to school together. Edward and I would see His Grace during school holidays at Warwick Abbey. As you can imagine, cricket games were quite intense." The men at the table all laughed in agreement.

"Kentwood, do you still speak with the now Earl of Warwick, Shelton?" Millington asked.

"Indeed, I do. Shelly married last year to Lady Annalyn Pennock. Currently, they have taken residence at Brewer House in town," responded Kentwood.

Miles asked, "Pray tell how is the Dowager Countess? Rumor has it she is a notorious flirt amongst society and has many lovers."

Rolling his eyes at Miles, Millington interjects, "Kentwood, forgive my brother. He tends to worship all women of every rank, shape, size, and age, and has a talent to say the most inappropriate things during an intimate dinner conversation." Millington glared at Miles.

Putting his glass of wine down, Kentwood chuckled and said, "No worries. Lord Miles is correct. She does flirt with everyone. It is all in good jest. According to Warwick, the Dowager Countess spends most of her time helping other widows adjust to their new circumstances. She has established a particular type of group that helps war widows. I am relieved she has found a purpose."

"I wish I could be more acquainted with the family. The Countess sounds marvelous. Edward, perhaps next time we are in town, you can make an introduction," Franny said as she sliced her tender venison dressed with herbs and a brown sauce.

"Mayhap, Lord Kentwood could help with your request. Miles and I have a strong relationship with two of her sons, but not so much with the Dowager Countess herself," said Millington.

Kentwood said, "I would be happy to acquire a meeting for you. Just send me a message when you are coming to London."

Franny was curious if perhaps Kentwood and Countess Warwick were more than just simple acquaintances, maybe even lovers. For some reason, the notion made her steam with jealousy. *What is wrong with me?*

Millington and Lord Miles spent many holidays and breaks from school with the Earl of Warwick and his ever-growing Brewer clan. The Honorable Robert Brewer, the third son, was a dear friend of Millington's, and the Honorable William Brewer, the fourth son, was best mates with Miles.

"There are so many Brewer children that they just go by numbers. No daughters. I'm not sure which is worse - that many sons or that many daughters. Either way you must secure their futures. I am amazed how the sons who are out in society are very successful and prospering. I believe William has an investment in a shipping company. Amazing at such a young age," Kentwood noted.

Miles perked up. "Yes, Warwick's sons, who number three and four, Edward and I are business partners with them. We have established a shipping company, respectively named Lane Brewer Shipping, and commence in exports and imports of non-living things. We do not cross the Atlantic nor partake in any slave trade."

Miles resisted further discussing slavery and the workings of plantations across the Big Pond, instead he focused his speech on his gratitude for his sister. "Franny plays a key role in the success of Lane Brewer Shipping. Her wisdom and ingenuity are priceless."

Miles raised his glass to Franny and toasted, "To our dearest sister, Francesca. Edward and I are forever in you service and we adore you."

Everyone but Kentwood chimed in, "Here, here!"

Franny had become more and more intriguing to Kentwood – more like an enigma. She was not like the rest of the *ton*. The more he learned about Franny, the more he tumbled hopelessly in love with her. Perhaps not exactly love. Maybe it was lust. More likely it was a mixture of feelings - like a third besotted, a third disgust, and a third lust. Kentwood was confused.

"Please expound if you will, what kind of imports and exports? I am hoping to learn how other revenue streams can benefit my estates during my time here. You were so young when you took over the family title and yet one of the most powerful and wealthiest Lords of the Realm. It's quite an accomplishment. Afterall you are called the Young Stoic Duke, and as I was recently reminded, I am merely the Adorable Duke."

Franny choked on her carrot and started drinking down her wine to help unlade the culprit. "Pardon me, that carrot proved most wicked to my person just then. No worries, all is right again." She tried to calm herself.

Millington gave his sister a puzzled observation and said, "Your Grace, I direct the question to my sister. I've only taken over operations of the ducal assets in the past year. Franny has overseen everything since our father's passing five years ago."

Clearing her throat and still slightly recovering from the wayward vegetable, Franny bluntly stated, "Olive oil. We import olives." With a hand on her upper chest and the other hand pouring wine down her throat, she continued, "We then manufacture various products using the olives and distribute them throughout the land. For a fee, we export whatever goods need passage to Italy, as long as the products are non-living as Miles previously stated."

Kentwood realized Franny's sun-kissed-like skin was from perhaps her Roma heritage. How scandalizing. *Where does she get the merit to insult me when it is she who is the bastard gypsy?* Again, Kentwood's curiosity got the best of him, and he asked, "Miss Lane, do you have ties with Italy through your Roma ancestry or is your mother's side completely unknown?"

The room went completely still and silent.

Fuck, I did it again. Saying stupid things that only get me into trouble. Kentwood's shoulders sagged a bit upon discovering his mistake.

Miles put his fork full of food down and his mouth gaped open. Franny looked down trying to keep her composure. Millington's ears turned the color of Franny's red dress and his eyes squinted in disgust right at Kentwood. Inhaling a deep breath and with a low, scratchy voice Millington spewed a warning, "Kentwood, you are here as my guest. My guests do not insult my family, nor do they ask such personal questions when you are acquaintances of mere hours. This is the second time today that I have had to speak to your person in such discourse. I will remind you that I do not care if our families have been great allies in the past, I will draw blades if needed."

"Caro Dio aiutami!" Franny exclaimed.

Franny knew she must act with haste to avoid bloodshed, and dessert had yet to be served. She dearly loved Cook's lemon sponge cake and would hate to miss out on it because of silly men trying to vie for whom had the biggest tailfeathers. "Dearest Edward, you are so sweet." Then turning to Kentwood, Franny addressed, "My brothers are very protective of me – almost to a fault. I am very proud of my heritage. It is not Roma, although I would be proud of that as well, and I can regard how that conclusion may be made. My mother was Italian. Her family has a vast amount of land with rows upon rows of olive trees. About four years ago, I was reacquainted with my mother's family. Miles traveled to their estate and learned everything about olives. Now we have formed a great and lucrative business venture together."

"Mama Maria's Hair Elixir?" Kentwood asked.

With a delightful smile Franny responded, "Yes, that is one of our products. Olive oil is great for skin, hair, and for cooking. It's taken England quite by storm. Very popular with the *ton*. As you stated previously, the Earl of Warwick needed additional funds with all those sons and granted monies to William and Robert to invest and help oversee the shipping operations."

Kentwood noticed the change in the air and used the moment to regain some respect from Millington and declared, "I am in awe of you, Miss Lane. Please forgive my ignorance."

Franny stared at Kentwood, whose apology was most sincere. *His children really would be beyond cuteness.* Blushing from Kentwood's comment, Franny turned to Millington and said, "Let's have dessert and champagne in the music room. Mix it up a little this evening. Would that be all right with you Edward?"

"Yes, sister. That sounds like a perfect notion. Let's depart to the music room." Millington stood and motioned for the dinner party to exit.

Upon entering the music room, Kentwood was taken aback by the massive instrument ensconced in the corner. It was the most glorious grand piano he ever saw. It appeared to be constructed entirely from one piece of mahogany. The dark wood was garnished with branches representing an olive grove. The light, blush pastels of the room made the instrument stand out even more. Coming alongside Kentwood, Franny quietly spoked,

"Bartolomeo Cristofori."

Kentwood stared at the piano. "Who?"

Franny explained, "Bartolomeo Cristofori, the creator of the grand piano, personally constructed and designed this very instrument you are gawking at. The Italians are acclaimed for more than just olives and wines."

"You forgot to say beautiful women. Italians are known for more than just olives, wines and beautiful women, Miss Lane." Kentwood whispered to Franny as he stared at her.

Blushing, Franny could feel her body instantly heat up. She cast her sight onto Kentwood and saw he was leering at her with the eyes of a roughish rake. She felt something strange stirring inside. A sense of "need" for Kentwood. The comment about Italy having beautiful women was directed right to her and she couldn't help but glow. This had never happened before – Franny was not sure how to handle a man's attention. She can't like him. She must detest him and his family for all eternity. They were responsible for destroying her mother's happiness. Franny broke the trance she was under and went to the piano and played.

Kentwood whispered to himself, "Easy Little Buddy. Easy. Don't make me think about crazy obtuse Queen Anne running naked with her stupid rabbits trough St. James Square again." He shivered at the thought. Kentwood listened to the flawless music Miss Lane effortlessly played. It sounded like a very difficult selection from Bach's Goldberg Variations. She was transformed into another world when she played. *Such passion.* Her long, elegant fingers flowing along the keys with such ease was a sight to behold. He pictured those very fingers gently, yet firmly grasping his shaft and stroking him. *Why can't I stop thinking of her in such a sexual matter? What is with this woman?* Franny was penetrating every part of Kentwood's body, from his mind to his heart to his groin. Little Buddy was affected by Franny's piano skills.

Bloody, Christ Almighty! Kentwood loosened his neckcloth, hoping it would cool down the heat radiating through him. He made eye contact with Miss Lane and lifted his glass to her. She sweetly smiled at him and played on.

At the end of the evening Franny bid good wishes to her brothers then turned to Kentwood and said, "Good night. Uhm… I hope you experience a restful sleep." She was nervous. *What kind of adieu was that? I hope you experience a restful sleep. I sound like a fool.*

Taking Franny's hand in his and kissing the top of her palm at the wrist, "Good evening to you, Miss Lane. You play masterfully and I hope you grace us with another concert soon."

The man was undoing her, little by little.

Chapter Three

"*Yes. Please, don't stop,*" *begged Franny. She sensed his breathing increasing and the slight moans that left his body accelerated the vibrations of the glorious tingles filling her. To have this strong, magnificent naked body on top of her, holding her tight has if he would lose his very life if they parted, was how Franny dreamed lovemaking would feel. She leaned into him, inhaling the scent of sandalwood and vanilla. His cheeks pressed against hers. "Oh, oh, please don't stop," Franny pleaded as she was about to reach her crescendo. Her insides exploded with a heavenly sensation that was on a different emotional and sensual level. She never wanted it to end. She turned her head to face him, but it wasn't Blake.*

Kentwood!

Franny screamed out loud in her sleep. Her lady's maid rushed into the room. "Milady, you are having a one of your nightmares again." Her lady's maid, Cecilia, had been with Franny since she came to her father's house. Patting Franny's back Cecilia consoled Franny further, "Take a deep breath milady. That's it. All is well. You are safe. I will go fetch some warm milk to help settle your nerves."

"Ah, yes… a nightmare." *Certainly, did not resemble one. What is going on? I can't possibly have feelings for that man.* "Thank you, Cecilia."

With the increased heat and wetness eluding between her legs, Franny would daresay the dream was no nightmare. A bath in the morning will be most needed. For Franny, an inner conflict was unfolding – a battle between her heart and her mind. She could not understand the affections she had for Kentwood. Her heart and sexual core voted to ravish the man, but her mind held Franny back from letting go. Afterall, it was his family that ruined her childhood and Kentwood could be of that same evilness. The wanton dream proved, beyond a doubt, that Franny could not deny that she was attracted to the Duke of Kentwood and in an almost animalist style. Never before had a man unraveled her so.

Cecilia returned with the warm milk, further soothing Franny. No words spoken. Franny drifted back to sleep as Cecilia gently rubbed her back.

Seated on the bench that belonged to the grand piano, he was holding onto a beautiful rump pressed down on the keys. He brought his mistress to straddle him. The swaying of her body hitting the keys almost sounded like parts of Beethoven's Moonlight Sonata. As his cock glided into her sweet, wet canal of bliss, she wrapped her arms around him and started to ride him slowly. Seated on top of him, she rocked back and forth in a smooth, tantalizing rhythm. He grabbed one of her slender, powerful thighs with one hand and the other cupped her perfectly sculpted breast. With his thumb he lightly teased her excited nipple in a circular motion. Her head dipped back reeling in the joyful lure of her approaching climax. He pressed into her with an embrace and inhaled the sweetness of her being – the scent of lavender and lemon.

"You are so beautiful. Please don't stop. You feel incredible. Come for me. Look at me. I want to see you," Kentwood said as he tried to fathom how her skin could feel so soft and velvet like. He turned to her face as she looked at him with loving, passionate green eyes slightly covered by the deepest black, lavish hair. He cupped his hands to her face and moved the veil of hair. Oh, Bloody Hell!

Miss Lane.

Kentwood bolted straight up in his bed, his breathing labored, heart beating faster than he could ever remember, and then realized it was a just dream. It was at that time he noticed his Little Buddy thought it wasn't a dream and made a creamy mess all over the bedding. *What the fuck? It's like I'm green and fourteen again.* Kentwood was slowly discovering that Miss Lane was far from being some common chit. *She must be a witch and has cast a spell on me.*

Unable to fall back to sleep and noticing the sun starting to rise, Kentwood decided a morning ride would be the best solution to rid Miss Lane from his thoughts. There was no way he was going to let that disobedient, headstrong, unpolished, unruly woman entrap him.

"Cecilia, I am going to go for a ride. This morning's sun is very enchanting indeed and I must soak my life in it," Franny declared.

"Very well milady, I will have your riding habit ready immediately."

Franny needed to ride for a few reasons that morning. First, she needed to rid her mind of last night's sinful dream with Kentwood. Second, she needed an excuse to bathe and wash away the moist evidence that was embedded in her valley from the delectable dream.

Blake, always the tentative groomsman, was tending to the horses at the early hour. He greeted Franny with a surprised smile and brought Mouse to her. "Glorious morning for a ride, Miss Lane."

Not looking at the man, still trying to wrap her mind around the dream, Franny responded, "Indeed, it is Blake. Thank you for having Mouse ready. I plan to open him up on the lanes today."

The stallion slightly pulled forward in anticipation of the forthcoming gallop. Franny noticed one of her brother's horses was missing. Another thoroughbred, with a very stubborn personality that produced a ride as if you were part of the wind itself. Only an experienced rider could handle him. "Blake, daresay where is Maximus?"

"The Duke of Kentwood is with Maximus as we speak. Appears you and the Duke are of the same mind this morning, Miss Lane." Blake glanced at Franny with a devilish smile and gave her a wink. Franny pouted and let out a slight growl in discord. Blake couldn't help but chuckle. Franny vowed to herself that she would have to avoid contact with Kentwood at all costs. Yet, she had to remain steady to all others so no one would detect the disturbance that swelled within her.

Once out on the lane, Franny let her hair down and urged Mouse into a flying sprint. The power of his hoofs made the earth shake. She clinched her legs to him to hold on. Franny found an inner power being able to control and stay on her beloved horse when they reached dangerous speeds. It was freeing. Easing up on the reins, Mouse paced down into a steady trot. Suddenly the ground was coming to life, Mouse was agitated, and Franny could feel the rumbling of the oncoming intruder in her chest. The monstrous hoofs of Maximus approached, which could only mean that Kentwood was closing in on her.

Oh drat!

"Good morning, Miss Lane! I see we are of the same mind and enjoying a good run as the sun rises. Best to get out now, it looks like rain will be setting in."

Franny could not help but stare at Kentwood. He was absolutely yummy. He had the most excellent seat even though it wasn't his personal horse. Franny glanced down at the Mouse's mane, trying to avoid all eye contact. Forcing a smile, she said, "Good morning. How are you handling Maximus? Is he being kind to you? He can be a bit testy."

Kentwood couldn't bring his eyes to venture from Franny. The way she was leaning on the horn of the saddle was simply tempting. He was picturing her riding him and leaning her fists into his chest to keep herself upright as she climaxed on top of him. Kentwood suddenly felt hot and started to loosen his necktie. He adjusted his seat to hopefully deter his Little Buddy from making an unwelcome rising appearance.

"Yes, he is a most spirited one. I relish the challenge. Your brother's stables are most impressive." Kentwood then eyed a stream a few paces away and suggested, "Perhaps our steeds are in need of refreshment. Will you do me the honor of taking a turnabout the grounds while they rest?" Kentwood hopped down from the saddle and held the reins of Maximus and Mouse, waiting for Franny to dismount. *It's over. I'm in a trance. She has enraptured me most completely. I am a doomed man.*

Franny gently lifted herself up and off of Mouse. In a church mouse of a voice she answered, "Yes, a walk will be most pleasant." She kept her head down as they led the horses to the babbling stream.

Offering his arm, Kentwood looked at Franny, "Please, tell how your family acquired such impressive horseflesh?" He gave Franny a boyish grin that offered a glimpse of his dimples.

When she wrapped her arm around his and held his forearm with her hand, she discovered the roping of his muscles. Franny paused for a brief second and closed her eyes in an effort to compose her being. *If I just didn't have that damn pleasurable dream about him, I would be fine at this moment.*

Settling her eyes on the horizon, Franny stated, "Our father would purchase four-year old stallions before they went to auction at Tattersalls. He would watch the Derby races and make offers to acquire the horses that didn't win and were about to be retired." Franny patted the Duke's forearm and continued, "Father hand an inkling that those horses would make the perfect riding companions. For the most part, he was right."

Intrigued by the conversation, Kentwood asked with a chuckle, "For the most part he was right? Please elaborate." As they continued the walk, he put his free hand upon Franny's hand that rested on his forearm. They walked as if they had been married for years – so naturally.

Franny almost stumbled when the warmth of his hand besieged hers. Wetness pooled between her thighs. *Keep it together,*

Franny. You can do this. He is an arse of a man, and you hate him. Don't forget. Franny responded, "Yes, the horse such as the one you chose to ride this morn, has a tendency to throw riders off. Especially when he gets wet. The dolt doesn't care for rain, or snow, or streams, or even mud for that matter. He is most odd in that fashion."

"Dooley noted. I will be careful to avoid, well… to avoid just about everything at this time of year while riding him," Kentwood nervously said.

Franny laughed with a small, light snort. Mortified, she put her gloved hand to her mouth to stop her actions. "Yes, this time of year I refer to it as the Mud Season."

Kentwood found Franny's sweet mishap of a laugh very charming. With a big smile of admiration, he asked Franny, "Why have I not seen you in town for the season?"

With that question, Franny's appearance changed to more of melancholy. Kentwood immediately regretted the question. *Fuck. Fuck. Fuckity, Fuck. I am such an ignoramus dope. Always saying the wrong things. Ugh!* Seeking to repair the damage he caused, Kentwood offered, "Forgive me. How impertinent of me. I say the darndest words sometimes. I am afraid it is a most unbecoming trait of mine."

Without thinking, Franny quietly said in a somber voice, "It is fine. Truth be told, it was my decision. I attended a few balls and dinners in the past when my brothers needed to make connections. The number of stares I received was quite unsettling and then there were the gossipmongers and scandal sheets. I realized, very early on, that the *ton* was never going to accept me." Franny paused, and for the first time since their walk started, she looked directly into Kentwood's eyes. Her own eyes welled with tears, and she painfully stated, "In their view, I am nothing more than a dastardly product of some foreigner who wished to gain a more lucrative life in England by offering her womanly services to a Lord of the Realm."

Taking the tip of his thumb, Kentwood wiped away the lone tear trinkling down Franny's cheek. His touch felt like a feather upon her skin – so caring. His eyes filled with empathy and compassion, as if he could feel the pain she felt. "In my experience, the busybodies of the upper tier are indeed some of the unhappiest of people. They see an intelligent and stunning woman like you and are immediately struck with jealousy and rage. All they can use are their worthless, evil words. I am sorry that happened to you."

He cupped her face with both hands, his thumb gently caressed her temple. Franny was lost in his eyes. The neigh of one of the horses snapped Franny into form. Shaking, Franny stepped back to exit the closeness between her and Kentwood. Observing the gathering clouds in the distance, Franny cleared her throat and said, "Yes, uhm… it seems like a rain may be upon us very soon. Best to get back to the stables. One thing I detest is cold mixed with rain." She whistled for Mouse to come to her.

Still in shock at what occurred, Kentwood replied, "Yes, I hope it is a good pour down so you can discover how successful the irrigation project is. I would like to be with you when you draw your conclusions after the rain. Do you mind if I join you, and your brother of course?"

Swinging her leg over her horse, Franny raised herself to be seated on the saddle. She answered, "Not at all. Now, I had best be back. Much to do." Franny turned Mouse and headed back to the stables. She needed to depart as quickly as possible. She detested the man but yet wanted his mouth all over hers. She was going mad.

Kentwood pleaded with Maximus like he was bargaining a trade at the docks, "Well, old chap, we best get back ourselves before you melt in the downpour. I fear the rain will engulf us. If you keep me alive, I will give you a delicious apple as a reward."

As soon as Franny dismounted Mouse and directed the beast to his stall, the heavens opened, and Franny got her wish for what appeared to be a daylong event of an early spring torrential rain. A wicked smile came across her face. Kentwood was still out there, surely soaked to the bone, and with a mad horse on his hands. Maximus did not like to get wet. She prayed he had excellent horsemanship skills, but also wished that he might take a light fall into a mud puddle. Imagining the Adorable Duke covered in mud brought an evil grin to her face. Franny conversed with Mouse, "There you go my darling. All brushed." Franny nuzzled her forehead to Mouse's neck. The horse in kind wrapped his head around Franny as if he were hugging her. "How

about some scrumptious oats for my good boy?" Mouse trembled with
cold causing Franny's body to shiver as well. She didn't realize the air
was as brisk as it was. She could see mist escaping the nuzzles of the
other stalled horses as they breathed.

Thankfully, during the previous year, Millington improved the
stables of Audrey Manor by installing additional fireplaces. Recent
winters, and even summers, were severely cooler than in the past.
Franny went to the fires and stocked them with kindling, hoping to
warm the stables a bit. She stretched her arms out closer to the fire to
warm her cold hands. That's when she heard the frantic dashing of
Maximus and an alarmed Kentwood yelling, "Whoa! Whoa, I say! You
crazy buffoon!" Franny tried her best not to laugh but it was no use.

Kentwood made it back to the stables but not before the cold
rains appeared. It seemed Maximus wanted to get back as fast as
possible and gave Kentwood the ride of his lifetime. He was thankful
to be back, even though his topcoat was soaked, and a chill was setting
in – his two feet were safely on the ground and his neck was still
attached to his body. A whisky was in order after that hellish ride. He
directed Maximus to the stall and took his coat and neckcloth off, then
shook both the coat and his hair free of the dripping rain. "Well, I guess
I will not be in need of a bath now. Thank you, Maximus, for the ride
and for not killing me." He gave the horse the promised apple.

A sweet giggle came from the other end of the stable. *Miss
Lane.* The sound warmed Kentwood to his core. When his gaze saw
her, an unknown force mystically attacked him. Franny took his breath

away. Keeping himself from staring at her beauty he said, "Hello, Miss Lane. Did you fare better than I and miss the rain?"

Sheepishly she smiled and answered, "Yes. I see you were not so fortunate." Her face winced as if she were in pain, she could tell Kentwood was cold. He stood there with his black riding boots, tan breeches and his shirtsleeves rolled to just below the elbows. The soaked white shirt he dunned created a see-through material, exposing his exceptional, muscular body. He was insanely beautiful. She just starred. Realizing this, Franny shook herself and tried to grab the feeding bag for Mouse. The bag was placed just within her fingers' reach. It had to be high so Mouse wouldn't grab it and tear it to shreds.

Kentwood came to her rescue, "Let me help. Sometimes being a tall oaf can be useful." He strutted over to where Franny was, taking notice of the warmth of the fires as he passed by them.

Franny stretched her body and said, "It is no issue, I can reach it." She stopped trying to fetch the bag when she perceived that Kentwood's body was directly behind her. Both of their bodies faced the post where the feeding bag hung. Her body yearned to lean back against his chest. She heard him let out a sigh of frustration.

Kentwood wasn't thinking. He just wanted to help her grab the feed bag. With her body stretched out the way it was, her backside was highlighted. Kentwood witnessed her thin waist and how it gently flowed into the curve of her tight, scrumptious buttocks. Desperately wanting to touch her, he gently placed a hand on Franny's back - right at the swell of the spine before the waist.

Franny deeply inhaled, trying to calm herself. Her body became very warm from Kentwood's intrusion of her personal space. She slightly leaned back into him. He was cold. Briefly closing her eyes, she took a deep breath. His scent was of fresh rain and sandalwood. She was being pulled closer into his body.

Kentwood reached for the bag and Franny's fingers met his and intertwined them together. His forearm bared corded muscles. So divine. Both bodies froze. Franny turned to face him. His hand never left her backside. He leaned his head close to Franny's hair. Just like his dream, it smelled like lemon and lavender. Intoxicating. His nose slightly nuzzled into her hair. Kentwood leaned down and whispered in Franny's ear, "Where is your groomsman?"

Turning her face slightly to the side allowing her cheek to rub his, she softly spoke, "He has a few hours off every day to attend to his family. They just had their sixth child and Blake is a dear...." Franny lost her train of thought as she stared into his eyes, and then at his splendid lips. Without a sense of decorum, Franny took her hand from Kentwood and ran her index finger along his bottom lip, realizing she had no gloves on. His lip left a fuzzy impression on her finger. Time was standing still.

Blowing out a breath of frustration, Kentwood tried to hold back his want to ravish Franny. He no longer wished to fight it and shoved Franny into his chest and pressed down on her lips in a searing kiss. The heat they produced sent away whatever chill the rain had procured earlier. Kentwood did not relent but lashed kiss after kiss onto

Franny and she responded with as much intensity. She opened for him and drank in his tongue, matching his skills. He had never experienced a rapture like this. It was on a different level.

A large popping noise from the fire jolted Franny to her senses. She started to panic. *How can I be enjoying this? It is his family who hurt my mother. His family destroyed my childhood. Why must there be this absurd attraction between us?* With a foot braced up against the post behind her, Franny used all her power to shove Kentwood away to break the entanglement. She looked at him in complete shock. Touching her lips, she left and ran out into the rain, back to the dower house.

Catching his breath, Kentwood stood with his arms crossed, resting on his chest. He leaned his body against the stable entrance door, and he watched Franny fade into the distance. She never looked back. "Well, Little Buddy, we are in big trouble now." Kentwood was baffled. He wanted Franny more than any woman he had known – more than he ever thought possible. He would have to keep clear of being in Franny's presence. There was no feasible way he could be within an arm's reach of the woman and not catch fire.

Chapter Four

Escaping the rain, a soaked Franny stumbled into the dower house as if someone were chasing after her. She slammed the door and immediately rested her back and head against it, gasping for air. Cecilia rushed to see what the commotion was all about. "Miss Lane, are you alright? You seem as if your life is hanging from a limb."

Head down, Franny paced back and forth with her hand over her heart trying to calm her nerves. Her chest had slight pains in it. She repeated, "No. No. No. Oh, no."

Cecilia realized Franny was beyond distraught and became gravely concerned. "Do you need me to request the physician? I have been in your company for a mere eleven years and have never seen you suffer dyspnea. Have you been harmed? Please tell me what has happened so I can assist with efficiency. Has someone harmed you?!"

Still holding her hand to her heart, Franny took a deep breath and exhaled. She gained her composure, lifted her head, and said to Cecilia, "A bath will be needed. Perhaps something stronger than tea. Maybe some brandy, please. Thank you."

Not quite able to communicate fully, Franny allowed Cecilia to help rid her of the damp clothing. She slid into the warm bath water. Cecilia asked once again, "Do you require a physician?"

"No, my friend. I am unharmed. Just shaken." Franny allowed her body to rest in the bath. She touched her lips and recalled the incident with Kentwood in the stables. *I wish you didn't belong to that family, otherwise I would most willingly give myself to you.*

Clearing her throat, Cecilia instigated Franny, "Please address what transpired? You are shaken to your core! Why did you not wait at the main house or the stables until the rains ended? Forgive me. I am speaking out of line but it's only because I care."

Cecilia was the childless widow of the village livery master. She might be built like a waif, petite and short in stature, but Cecilia had the ability to command an army. Just shy of five and forty, she arrived at Audrey Manor at the same time Franny did - needing a change of perspective and way of life after her dear Ronnie passed from a most dreadful accident. He was trampled by horses. Ronnie had saved the lives of three young village children who were in the direct path of the stampede.

Franny's father thought Cecilia would make the perfect companion and maid for his daughter who would desperately need direction in her new world after being raised by nuns. He wanted to secure Cecilia's future as a sign of immense gratitude for her husband's valor. Steadfast and loyal, Cecilia loved Franny as if she was her own child. The child she never had. In return, Franny held onto Cecilia as the confidant she needed to get through life's trials and tribulations. "And I care for you dearest, Cecilia. Let us go and have refreshments. I will unfold today's events that thus brought me to this point of dismay."

Warming by the fire in the small library, the two women sat in silence for a brief time. The wait was cutting Cecilia into pieces, and she couldn't bear it any longer. Taking a sip of brandy she broke the stillness, "Let me guess, the Duke of Kentwood?"

Franny, in her white nightrail and pale blue wrapper, hair all down resting on her body drying by the fire, swallowed a gulp of liquid courage and answered, "Is it that obvious?"

Placing her glass on the tray, Cecilia let out a sigh. "Not very many are privy to the role his family played in the sadness bestowed upon your mother and you. Daresay, not even your brothers are informed. When I heard he was to stay at Audrey Manor for a month my knees almost gave out on me. To know what pain this may inflict upon you and the memories it might conjure. Talk to me."

Holding the sniffer in her lap with two hands, Franny stared into the golden concoction and said in a confused, shaky voice, "I am supposed to hate him. Despise him with every grain of my being. *Loathe* him. But he does something to me that I cannot explain. I look upon his face and all I want is for him to embrace me. Kiss me. At the same time, the idea of caring even a little for someone of his lineage makes me want to cast up my accounts. I tell myself that there is no ability for someone of his family to be warmhearted. His appealing face and captivating charms are just a façade hiding a monster underneath. What am I to do?"

Cecilia, in a motherly, sweet voice, lightly patted Franny's leg, "Milady, perhaps he is not a wolf in sheep's clothing. Perhaps he is kind and cordial. You can't transfer his grandfather's actions upon him and stay so vexed. Our Lord above says the son shall not bear the iniquity of the father."

"Perhaps you are correct. Still, I will uphold my guard until I discover his true person. It is so hard to understand how I can feel this way and yet have so much anger." Franny was relaxed and peaceful as she gazed into the warmth of the fire. With a slight smile she confessed, "He kissed me."

Upon hearing Franny's proclamation, Cecilia jumped up from her seat and paced back and forth before the hearthstone with her hand over her heart, looking as if she was suffering from angina. Fanning her hand in front of her face she started to mumble, "Oh. Oh. Oh, my. Oh, dear. Well, well… well that is most surprising to hear. Uh, how… how was the encounter?" Her voice slightly raised an octave with the question.

Franny, seated on a comfy, cushioned chesterfield wingback armchair reflected on the kiss. It was rather kisses than just one kiss.

When his luscious lips touched hers it sent a wave of heat through her body that produced a throbbing need in her nether region. She recalled the moist release between her thighs that resulted from the exchange. It was as if the dream of her and Kentwood coupling was real. She never felt anything like it. *Passion*. She was shocked at the want for more of him and the fear it gave her. How could she want something that seemed so wonderful, so natural, from a man that she had vowed to despise? Lightly touching her fingers to her lips, she replied to Cecilia's question, "Bloody magical."

The Duke of Kentwood, Lord Bennett David Wheeler, was at a loss of what to do for the first time in his five and thirty years. Well, maybe not the first time in his life, but definitely the first time with the dealings of a woman – especially one that pushed back his advances. There was never a time when a woman of any rank denied him. He was aware of his attractiveness, his status in society and his vast amount of money. Lots of money. The past few years, Kentwood solely concentrated on repairing the financial mess his father left him. Now he was as wealthy as Millington.

Part of his stay at Audrey Manor was to discover how the young Duke made so much revenue and was still held in such a high regard amongst the *ton* and commoners. It was rumored that Miss Lane ran the estates, yet he could not get close enough to her to have her disclose any information. The vixen detested him. He was baffled and did not understand what precisely he did to make her dislike him so. *Why does she have to be so damn beautiful?* Just the thought of his lips on hers awoke Little Buddy. Mayhap, Little Buddy was wiser than his own mind and heart in this matter.

Determined to have a civil conversation with Miss Lane and keep all provocative thoughts at bay, Kentwood set forth to the dower house on foot. Darkness will soon be setting in as the sun lowered into the horizon. It was a pleasant evening for a short stroll. The home was a lovely cottage. Dark brown bricks with two floors sprawled about on over an acre of land. The entrance mirrored the main house. Large oak doors with forestry scenes ornamentally carved into the frames. Unlike the roses around the main house, the dower house hosted rows of various lilacs and lavenders with ivy vines climbing the corners of the home. Even after the cold winter, you could see traces of purple and indigo colors. Simplistic beauty.

"Was that a knock?" Franny inquired about the sound, as she rested by the fire, indulging in a second glass of brandy.
"I will go inquire milady." Cecilia stopped her pacing and headed to the foyer.

She opened the door and discovered Kentwood. Then immediately shut it – right in his face. The sight of the gorgeous gentleman, along with Franny's recent confession of the kiss they shared sent the older lady into a panic mode. She took a deep breath, calmed her nerves, put a smile on her face, and opened the door.

"Pardon, please forgive me, Your Grace. I seem to have a sudden attack of the vapors. And well, that causes my hands to get slippery, you see, and I accidentally shut the door in your sweet face… I mean person." Cecilia kept her head down while speaking. She dared not make eye contact with the Duke after the embarrassing debacle.

Kentwood stood frozen and looking rather puzzled, with no notion of what to do. Clearly the woman before him was flustered. "May I call upon Miss Lane? I seek an audience with her."

"Yes, Your Grace. This way. Please follow me," Cecilia responded as she gestured for him to come within.

The inside of the cottage reminded Kentwood of his hunting lodge in Scotland. Large oak rafters jetted across the ceiling and the paintings of the Italian masters of Gentileschi, de Boulogne, and Bronzino lined the hallway walls. Upon entering the drawing room, Kentwood lost his ability to breathe when his eyes spotted Miss Lane. She looked like she belonged in one of the paintings from the hall. Her manner was like the ocean calm, with a drink lingering in the hand of the arm that rested upon the chair. Her hair was down, framing her face. She sat relaxed, dreaming into the light of the fire. He wondered if she was reminiscing of the feverish moment from the stables, for he had not stopped thinking about it since.

Cecilia took one step into the room and cleared her throat, "Milady, the Duke of Kentwood is here to see you."

Startled at the announcement, Franny immediately stood up and dropped her glass onto the plush, Axminister Rug. "Kentwood!"

Suddenly reminding herself she was scantily clothed under her robe, she looked at the front of her body and rubbed down her covering as if it would magically change into an appropriate day dress or evening gown.

"Please forgive me Miss Lane for not sending a note beforehand. I can come back another time." The Duke apologized and started to turn to leave.

Glaring at Cecilia with big eyes, Franny addressed Kentwood, "No. That is not necessarily. Pray forgive me. Your presence startled me. We do not receive many visitors here. Please sit. Would you care for a drink? Wine? Brandy? Whisky? Tea?" Franny was jabbering with nervousness.

"That would be lovely." Examining the refreshment cart, he declared, "Perhaps a brandy. Thank you."

Nervously, Cecilia fanned her face with her hand. She rushed to pick up the snifter that Franny dropped. "Oh my, the vapors are at it again. Sometimes it's hard being a woman. One moment you are just fine and right and the next you have the vapors." Not quite knowing how to leave the room, Cecilia announced, "Well, well, well. Yes. I... I must attend to these vapors. Ring if you need me. Tootles!" The woman scattered out the door like a crazed cat scampering after a mouse.

As Kentwood watched Cecilia leave, he spoke with a low, soft voice from the side of his mouth to Franny, "Is she mad?"

"No, she is not mad. Just different," said Franny with a suspicious look on her face, one eyebrow raised. "Although, I have never seen her act this way or suffer from the vapors before."

Franny poured herself and Kentwood some brandy. Kentwood took a seat in the chair that she just occupied. He swung his topcoat to rest on the chairback. He wore a white oxford shirt with the sleeves rolled up, reviling his forearms of strength. *Why does he have to show those impressive forearms?* His neckcloth was absent. He sat a bit slanted with one leg propped over the armrest. Franny was taken aback at his improper, relaxed person. With a thankful smile, Kentwood took the drink from Franny as she offered it to him.

"Must you smile at me?" Franny asked Kentwood with a perplexed grin.

In reply, Kentwood annoyingly stated, "Now I can't smile at you. I can't kiss you. I can't have a civil conversation with you. Please don't tell me that my eyes can't look upon you as well. Are you Medusa?"

Franny plopped down into the chair across from Kentwood and exhaled a big sigh. "Your smile is my undoing, not to mention your forearms. Pull your sleeves down. You call yourself a duke?" Waving her hand up and down at Kentwood she continued, "This is the most absurd way for a duke to sit in a chair."

Kentwood stood up and approached Franny with the most frustrated face. Leaning down on her as she sat in the chair, he drawled with intimidation, "What have I done to you to deserve this disrespect?

This aversion for my person? Never have I encountered someone who disliked me at first sight."

Franny scowled at Kentwood with a stoned face and abruptly stood to show she was not intimidated. Her push of physicality caused Kentwood to stand up straight. She stared at Kentwood and declared, "I do not have to respect you. I do not like you. You… your family… they disgust me."

Kentwood stepped back, shocked by her accusations. "What is this about? I assure you that I have no notion of how your hatred was born. But if my family was part of it, your answer will not surprise me."

Under his armor of beauty and grace, something greatly troubled Kentwood. His changed demeanor revealed a darkness of some kind. The Duke had inner demons to slay, there was no doubt of it. With Kentwood's slight admission of his family's uncouth behavior, Franny sensed there may be more to the history between the families than she once believed. It was feasible that Cecilia was correct about him. He may not be a wolf in sheep's clothing after all, perhaps he was even a victim. However, the anger that dwelled inside Franny was too great. She could never let this die. "Your grandfather is the root of this pain." Franny points her index finger into her chest. "He destroyed my mother's life, my childhood, and the love my parents had for one another. Along with my grandfather, the two of them drew alliances to make sure no Italian blood ruined the precious Millington lineage."

Puzzled, Kentwood said, "I fear I do not follow. You are a bastard, are you not? I beg your forgiveness for using the term, but it is the reality. Is it not?"

Taking a step back, Franny took a cleansing breath and upon the exhalation she decided to unlock the mystery for Kentwood. "When my father, Nathaniel, went on his Grand Tour, he was the second born son – the spare. He stayed longer in Italy than planned. Nathaniel fell in love with my mother, the beautiful Maria Gabriella Moretti. They married. Upon returning to England with his Italian bride, my father discovered his older brother died in a horse racing accident and that he was now the heir."

Franny started to slightly pace back and forth, using her arms and hands to conduct the orchestra of her story. She divested, "Well, you can't be married to an exotic if you are an heir to a dukedom. So, your grandfather and my grandfather came up with a scheme. They kidnapped my mother and sent her to Northumberland – locked her up in a cottage in the middle of nowhere. Then had someone write a letter in Italian to my father saying she could no longer live away from her homeland. The letter stated she returned to Italy."

Franny caught her breath, gulped down the rest of her drink and continued. "At the time, she did not realize she was with child. My father was heartbroken. England didn't recognize the marriage because it was performed by a Roman Catholic priest and on foreign land. My father was free to marry a proper English lady who would be the future

Duchess of Millington. So, since he thought his Italian bride betrayed him, he went on to marry again."

Franny stopped in front of the fireplace. Hands by her side, she stared into the flickering flames and continued in a most solace, quite voice, "I was born on a cold winter's day. We barely had enough to eat. I watched my mother shrivel up into nothingness. She died when I was eight. I did my best to care for her. Made the tea, biscuits, broth, kept the fires burning - whatever I could do for such a young child." Tears slowly trickled down Franny's face. She wiped them away with her sleeve. Recalling the horrific events of her childhood was never easy and she only shared them with Cecilia prior to this point. Why she decided to include Kentwood as a trusted acquaintance was beyond her.

She picked her head up, turned to Kentwood, and continued in a very nonchalant matter, "I sat with her dead body in that cottage for three days until the village midwife stopped by for her weekly visit. The next day, I was whisked away to a convent in Dorset. I can only imagine how much money my grandfather paid to have the nuns take me in and hide me from society. I was the only child on the premises. I never had anyone to play with. It was the loneliest childhood."

Kentwood's body shuttered, feeling as though all his blood had rushed out. He wasn't sure the last time he breathed as Franny recalled her upbringing. Using his elbow as an anchor to hold him steady, Kentwood leaned slightly into the large oak mantle of the brick fireplace. He knew what his loveless family was capable of, but this was beyond the pale.

Franny proceeded to explain how her mother was too embarrassed to reach out to her Italian family for aid. How her father's very English wife of the *ton* never became the Duchess of Millington. She died when Miles was two years of age. They had believed she was increasing with child again. It was not a babe but a type of internal growth that consumed her whole being – a cancer was what the doctor called it. The pain it brought her was too much. The Duchess took too much laudanum, by her own accord. On a sunny, beautiful afternoon she died while sleeping. My father found her with a sweet smile on her face and Miles sleeping in his dead mama's arms. She had gone onto a greater reward.

When Nathaniel inherited the dukedom, he discovered Franny's existence after stumbling upon correspondence between her grandfather and Kentwood's. It took him four years to find her. When he did, he brought Franny to Audrey Manor and spent the rest of his days making amends for his family's actions. He taught her everything about running the estates and she helped to raise her younger brothers.

Stepping forward towards Franny with full concern, Kentwood held back the water that was stinging his eyes. He reached for her hand. The wide sleeves of Franny's robe drifted up on her arm and allowed Kentwood to lightly caress Franny's forearm with his thumb. That's when he felt the scars. He witnessed small horizontal wisps crisscrossing her skin. He looked at the other wrist and was appalled at the sight of additional marks.

Franny frowned into Kentwood's eyes. Her eyes were dark with no emotion in them – the color of a torrent black sea. She answered the question he didn't ask, "Yes, while you had the perfect childhood climbing trees, fishing, and enjoying the love of two parents, I was beaten by the nuns at the abbey. They tried to cleanse the bastardy from me. In their eyes I was made with the blood of Satan. Right answer, wrong answer, it didn't matter. The stick came down no matter what."

All Kentwood wanted to do was hold her. He never felt so helpless. This beautiful creature before him was subject to such horrors and all because of his family. No wonder he enraged her. He wanted to make all the pain disappear, holding her until warmth infiltrated her heart once again. Kentwood slowly brought his hand up to her face and with the pad of his thumb he traced the bottom of her chin. He softly spoke very close to her ear, "Miss Lane, I am deeply sorry for the agony my family caused you. There is nothing I can do to change it. I just wish you didn't hold their actions against me. I knew nothing of this. It is not my person to live the way my father and my grandfather did. I am not like them. Please forgive me for being born of them." He tenderly kissed Franny on the cheek.

"I can never forgive you or your family," Franny angerly whispered. Even after Kentwood's delicate and caring plea for forgiveness, Franny could not find it in her heart to let go of all the anger and pain.

Lifting her chin with his fingers so her eyes met his, Kentwood asked in a seductive tone, "Tell me you didn't feel anything from earlier in the stables today? I know you did. I did. I have never experienced such a powerful impact on my being than the kiss we shared. We have something rare. Tell me you feel the same."

Franny glimpsed at his lips and then back to his eyes. She felt the same compelling drive during the kiss they shared, but Franny was stubborn and wasn't freed from the pent-up anger inside her. "I didn't feel anything but remorse and regret afterwards. It must be hard for the Adorable Duke of Kentwood to be denied. Hopefully, your ego won't suffer too greatly." *This is the most painful speech I have ever given. I do not want to hurt you. This pains me more than it will pain you. In the end, you will thank me. This is for the better.*

Shaking his head, he backed away from her. He exclaimed, "So I am to be punished forever then? You will deny yourself pleasure? Happiness? Perhaps, even love? All because of what my ancestors did? I am not responsible for their behavior!"
Kentwood noticed he was about to lose his temper.

"Please leave," Franny requested with a stare full of emptiness.

Kentwood brought his lips to hover just above Franny's. He gave a short growl then sweetly kissed Franny's forehead and exited the house. He was adrift in what had just come to pass. She will never experience the intimacy of love or happiness because she will not let her heart heal. That much enmity will break her soul into so many pieces that it would be deemed irreparable. He knew this to be factual and could only attest that he was fortunate to stop the darkness of his past from overtaking his own soul. Granted, it was a daily battle to not let the past creep out and claim the present, but perhaps there was a way he could help Miss Lane find some kind of peace – even if she vowed to hate him for all eternity.

Chapter Five

After a restless night of sleep and breaking her morning fast, Franny set out to walk about the estate and inspect the various water diversion projects. The morning sun was drying the nightly frost. The recent rains provided an excellent test and hopefully the endeavors proved successful in moving water to the more fertile soils. Along her walk she spotted Kentwood by the very same pond she first came to be in his bewildering presence. He was swimming on that rather cold and brisk morning. Apparently, he was an early riser such as herself. Feeling much remorse for her behavior the night before, she went towards him to offer an apology and explanation for her actions. Franny had a habit of letting her inner resentment get the best of her and cloud her judgement.

Leaning against the tree where his clothing hung, she marveled at his body. Instead of remorse, lust took over her being. She longed for his Herculean arms to wrap around her. She yearned to lay her head on his chiseled chest. He was the most able-bodied form of art she ever laid eyes on. Her mouth opened slightly at the discovery of it all.

"Are you going to stand there and stare at my fine physique all day?" Kentwood teased her as he stood in the water with his chest exposed and a boyish smile highlighting those irresistible dimples and with his caramel brown eyes flirting.

Casting all thoughts of malice aside, Franny begged herself to be friendly. *Remember Cecilia's words from the night before - son shall not bear the iniquity of the father.* With her arms crossed to help keep warmth in, she taunted him with a vixen stare and grin. "It's a bit cold for a swim. I was hoping to stumble upon you this fine morning. Much to my delight, I find you looking very vulnerable at this moment."

"Forgive me, sometimes my Scottish blood desires a cold and refreshing soak." For some reason, his body wasn't a bit cold. The sight of Miss Lane warmed him in the wickedest of ways. Forgetting all rules of decorum, Kentwood continued, "And Miss Lane, I am not the vulnerable one right now. I am afraid you are though, for I am about to come out of the water as naked as the day I was born."

Franny did her best to not show any stupefaction and channeled her inner minx. "Please do proceed. It will be *most delicious* to see the entirety of you. For you are a most heavenly built being."

Temptress! What the bloody hell? Kentwood couldn't believe what he was hearing, but he liked it. No, he loved this side of Miss Lane. She was wild, clever, fun, and flirtatious. Never one to turn down a dare, Kentwood slowly strutted as if he was Poseidon emerging from the water to seek out his Amphitrite. He never took his eyes off Miss Lane, who didn't have a look of trauma about her. Instead, she was studying him with a face of intrigue. That's when he realized the water was very cold and cold water makes certain parts of the body shrink.

"Just to clarify, the water is rather cold, and my Little Buddy usually appears in a more grandiose matter when it's warmer." Kentwood couldn't help blurt out the ridiculous statement. *What was I thinking by saying that? I am a dolt.*

"Your Little Buddy?" Franny laughed with a slight snort, covering her mouth with her hand.

He smiled at Franny, showing his dimples and his eyes sparkled with playfulness. "You know… my manly bits. My Little Buddy. Please turn your back for I wish not to cause you to swoon."

Smirking, Franny turned her back from him. She continued to be bold and with a flirtatious voice said, "You call *it* your Little Buddy? Well, I daresay your Little Buddy looks beautiful to me."

Kentwood yelled, "No peeking! Do not turn back around until I say."

Breaking the tension further, she decided it was the perfect time to apologize. Still with her back to him, she lifted her head a bit higher and cleared her throat. "I wish to apologize for my harsh words last evening. You did not deserve them. It was not your fault and I realize that now. I should not pass the sins of your grandfather unto you. It was very bad form of me. I wish to begin our acquaintance anew. Please forgive me." She wished to add, *"Oh and I find it so adorable you call your manly bits, Little Buddy. You truly are the Adorable Duke."*

"Apology accepted," Kentwood said as he hurriedly put his legs into his trousers. He felt like his body had met some sort of collision at the hearing of her atonement. She had a heart after all. *What to do with this new knowledge?* Kentwood was hopelessly falling for this beautiful, exotic, intelligent, and most perplexing creature.

As Franny turned to face Kentwood, the air left her lungs as she tried not to gasp. He was truly a most gorgeous man. With his hair a wet mess, he was bent over retrieving his shirt. That's when she noticed all the markings on his back. Some more red than others. The lines formed valleys and hills and oddly enough it reminded her of the Scottish terrain she once saw as a child. So many scars. She was at a loss for words. Franny stood frozen in shock of what was the most painful and disturbing flesh she'd ever seen. Not disturbing in an ugly way but in a way that made her heart leap from her chest because she could not fathom the physical pain he must have endured. She wanted to wrap him in her arms and offer comfort. Much like a lovely mother would for her child who just scrapped a knee.

As he was bent down to grab his shirt, Kentwood glanced up and noticed Franny's toes pointed towards him. She had turned around before he said she could. *Does this woman ever obey?* Her silence indicated she could see the monstrosity of scars weaved into his backside. Not the Adorable Duke as everyone thought. He sternly said in a low voice, "I did not say you could turn around."

Not knowing what to do, Franny panicked. She wasn't terrified by the sight. She was horrified at whatever had caused Kentwood the pain and agony of the scars. She was paralyzed with her mouth agape, tears started to pool in her eyes, and her breathing became labored. She said the only thing she could think of at the moment, "I... I was unaware you participated in the war. Where did you see battle?"

Fiercely, Kentwood put his shirt over his head and stepped towards her. He was looking down on her. The sheer terror upon her face was all Kentwood saw. She had seen his secret. He was damaged goods to her now – a monster, a most undesirable person to gaze upon. He saw the disgust in her eyes, and it angered him. His temperament turned thorny and the beast within him lashed out with a sarcastic, dangerous tone, "Oh, those scars. Hideous, I know. The battle I fought will never be resolved. If you recall our conversation from last evening, the scars are from that wonderful, perfect childhood you described me as having."

Kentwood's face was insufferably close to hers. He wanted to tame the spiteful monster that was emerging from him by kissing Franny senseless, but it was no use. The reminder of his past was something he had never completely conquered. To avoid any more wounding words he simply said, "Good day, Miss Lane." Then walked away, never looking back.

Franny had seen pain, not just her pain but the pain of others. She can relate to having a constant reminder of scars on one's body. She witnessed her mother's pain caused by losing a great love, the physical pain of her own beatings by the nuns, and her father's pain of regret for not knowing his daughter existed. But Kentwood's pain was different. It was dark. It was something that she felt he couldn't escape. Perhaps it haunted his dreams at night. It was a pain that caused anger and emptiness. Much like the pain she was trying to rid herself of - the animosity towards his family.

That evening, Franny met with Millington to converse about business before dinner. They sat across from each other at the double-pedestal partner's desk made of the finest oak with carving details matching the main entrance doors of Audrey Manor – the White Cliffs of Dover. Secret doors blanketed the desk inside and out and could only be opened by solving the puzzles surrounding them. Their father was a child at heart and dearly loved puzzles. His most beloved books and wooden puzzle boxes were on display in the study. The four large, narrow windows that towered from floor to ceiling displayed a magnificent, heavenly sunset. Rembrandt couldn't match the artistic stroke of what God was painting at that moment. Sipping her wine, Franny inquired, "What do you know about the Duke of Kentwood?"

Peering up from the papers he was studying, Millington said, "That is too vague a question, dearest sister. It is like if I asked you at the breakfast table, 'How did you enjoy your day?' When it has not yet begun. Please be specific. What exactly do you wish to unearth? I suspect you have developed some sort of *affection* for him. It seems all the ladies who meet him, do. Oh God, please do not say you are besotted?"

Surprised by how well her brother saw right through her, Franny did her best to uphold her guard. She did have feelings for Kentwood but wasn't sure what those inclinations were. It was something she's never experienced. "What is with you and the word, besotted?" Shaking her head and refocusing on the subject once again she questioned, "He's childhood. Do you know anything about it? He seems, well... rather lonely."

Millington leaned back in his chair and threw his booted feet upon the desk. He sipped his whisky trying to figure out how to best answer his sister's question. Curiously looking at Franny with one brow slightly higher than the other he said, "What I heard is via the lips of Robert Brewer." Robert was the third son of the Seven Sons of Warwick. "We spent quite a few holidays from university at the estates of Warwick. Kentwood was friends of the Earl's eldest son, the heir, who was the only child from Warwick's first marriage. From what Kentwood divested over dinner the other night, he was not always an only child. He had an older brother. There was the heir and Kentwood was the spare. Some kind of tragic accident occurred when Kentwood was young, perhaps nine or ten years of age. Rumor has it was a drowning. His brother perished and Kentwood became the heir. Other than that, I know very little. Expect that his father was a Cad of the First Water. Kentwood never spoked of his father, and I believe their relationship was non-existent."

Suspecting there was more to Franny's inquisition, Millington asked, "Sister, has something happened between you and Kentwood? Has he harmed you? His reputation is that of a rake and his notorious temper." Raising his hands in the air with a perplexed face he continued, "Not sure why he is called the Adorable Duke."

Franny let out a tiny giggle. She thought to herself, something must have happened to him in childhood. What a terrible tragedy to lose an older brother at such a young and impressionable age. Kentwood probably respected his older brother and worshipped the ground he walked on. Nothing can prepare a person for such an event – the loss of a loved one. *But the scars. By what virtue does a child receive such marks? Perhaps self-inflicted?* Franny recalled the priests at the abbey whipping themselves, practicing a form of flagellant. Whatever or whomever inflicted Kentwood's scars, the events also left scars on his innermost being as well. Franny had to stop thinking about it or her eyes would give her away and start shedding tears for Kentwood, then her brother's suspicions would be validated.

Millington, witnessing Franny deep in thought, spoke, "Kentwood spent a great deal of time with Warwick and his family. They treated him as if he were one of their own." Millington knew Kentwood's father was worthless as a parent and as a Lord of the Realm. He continued, "He's father was never one to bend to new ways of running estates, nor did he want to dabble in the latest infrastructure. Kentwood inherited a crumbling domain. He is fixing each property one at a time. It's no wonder he is making the best of his stay here to learn different ways of improving the ducal coffers. You must do better to show him. I beg of you to be kinder."

Franny stood and glided over to the windows, wine glass in hand. With one arm crossing over chest, she rested her elbow on it and drank her wine, breathing in the sunset sky with its mosaic of purple, pink and red colors. "No worries, dearest brother. I have already started to make amends for my appalling behavior. I do hope you forgive me for my lack of manners with the Duke."

Standing to join his sister in watching the sunset, Millington said, "No need for forgiveness. You have always had a cold demeanor with new acquaintances. I don't blame you, given your upbringing. Our properties would not be in the exceptional state they are in, if not for you. I am just thankful that you are here with us now. You are and will always be the most treasured of sisters that any brother could wish for."

Franny rested her head on the side of Millington's upper arm. A warm, sibling embrace of sorts. "Thank you, Edward, for being so wise for your age. I appreciate your guidance."

Millington's eyes started to water. To interrupt the moment of kindred spirit, he declared, "Well, enough of this sappiness. I'm famished. Let us see if dinner is ready to be serve."

Millington and Franny were not surprised to see their brother, Lord Miles, already seated at the dining table. The young man had the appetite and table manners of four giant Scots who just came home from a day of chopping down trees in the forest. With the three siblings seated, Kentwood came charging in – looking rather disheveled, even his neckcloth was loose. He appeared to be having a mental battle of sorts. Bennett reassured himself, "*I have no patience for this evening's dinner. Melancholy has taken over my being and I fear my temper will present itself in the most ugliest of ways. I must hold myself together and not be a rude guest.*"

Millington glanced at Franny as a reminder to be kind. As Kentwood stood at the doorway, Franny got up from her seat and approached Kentwood. Standing in front of him, she presented Kentwood with the most elegant curtsy. Looking directly at him, she said with an angelic voice, "Good evening, Your Grace. We are honored to have your presence here with us this evening. Please join us for dinner."

Lord Miles, seated to Millington's right side, stopped his soup spoon midair with his mouth wide open. He was shocked at Franny's impeccable manners since she rarely displayed them. Kentwood held his head a little higher and stared over Franny to avoid eye contact and said in a rather abrupt voice, "Thank you. I shall." Then took the seat next to Miles. Franny returned to her seat that was to the left of Millington.

Franny interjected, "Lord Kentwood, we have great news to share! Edward and I have inspected the new irrigation project and spoke with the tenants working on those lands. The smaller creeks created have successfully diverted water to the more fertile lands that once dried too soon during the growing season. We are anticipating a most bountiful harvest next season. Perhaps I can show you how the plan was implemented. Do you have time tomorrow?"

Staring at his soup and sipping it off the spoon, Kentwood replied with a voice that was cold as ice, "That would be adequate."

Recalling the events of earlier that day at the pond, Franny cast a glance of worry toward Kentwood. He appeared to have no emotion and talked in a monotone.

Kentwood looked up from his meal and emotionlessly spoke, "Millington, my ward and younger cousin, Lady Sophia Wheeler, will be traveling to Kent within a week's time. I am hoping it will be satisfactory with you if she resides at Audrey Manor while she visits. The repairs to Bayberry Hall are still undergoing. Perhaps Miss Lane can serve as chaperone when I am not present."

The way Kentwood spoke of his cousin revealed little of his affection for her. Perhaps she was a troubled girl that vexed him. Maybe it was the upcoming visit that put Kentwood into such a stupor.

"Of course, that is no issue. We will welcome Lady Sophia and I am sure Franny will be excited to have another female amongst us," said Millington. He was not quite sure what he agreed to.

"Yes, I look forward to having tea with Lady Sophia and sharing secrets. It will be a wonderful distraction," said Franny with a chipper voice trying to lift the mood.

Miles, with a mouth full of food blurted out, "Is she pretty?"

"Miles!" Both Millington and Franny exclaimed, giving Miles a disgraced cast.

Kentwood shot straight up out of his seat, still with no expression, almost as if he were bored of everything around him. "I apologize. I must excuse myself. I have been dealing with a megrim all day. I bid you good evening."

Kentwood gave a slight dip of the head to bow and left the dining room without making eye contact with anyone.

Miles, still eating, glanced between Millington and Franny, and asked, "Was it something I said?"

"Oh, do shut up, Miles," scorned Franny.

Chapter Six

Franny sat in her favorite chair by the fire in the library of the dower house, relishing a glass of wine. It was her reading chair that was home to a pillow that Franny made long ago. The embroidered stitching of a lavender field on the face of the pillow was created by her mother. It was the one piece of her that Franny was able to keep all these years. Recalling events from dinner, Franny was beside herself trying to figure out what troubled Kentwood. He appeared out-of-sorts at dinner. She desperately wanted to help him. It occurred to Franny that the resentment she kept inside her heart for Kentwood was slowly fading away. As for that kiss in the stables, she never knew a kiss could be that all-consuming. It made her feel like she was floating off her feet – like an untamed beast losing all control.

The more she conjured what tragedies Kentwood had experienced, most likely from the very hands of his father, the more she wanted to soothe his pain. *I am falling in love with him. Am I? Perhaps I just care for him on a deeper level, like I care for my brothers. But he makes me want more from him, something carnal.* Franny touched her lips recalling their passionate kiss. *Why did I stop that kiss? I am such a silly-nilly.*

A soft knock at the main door interrupted Franny's woolgathering. She had given her staff the night off. Franny was only wearing a chemise with a pastel blue housecoat tied at her midsection. With her feet bare and her hair brushed out for the night, she went to the foyer and opened the door.

Kentwood.

He was wearing no tie, black trousers, a white shirt with the first few buttons undone, a black vest, and a dark blue velvet coat. His hair was in disarray, yet Franny could not take her eyes off him. Her heart fluttered a few extra beats and her breathing increased. With a nervous smile, she offered the second curtsy of the evening, a record for Franny, and said, "Your Grace, do come in. What a pleasant surprise."

He stepped into the foyer. "I am sorry for not sending a note beforehand… again." Appearing lost, Kentwood looked around and noticed the house was quite silent. "Pardon me, but are you alone? I should leave. We can discuss this matter in the morning." He rubbed his hands on the sides of his trousers as if they were sweaty and in need of drying. *My God, she was ready for sleep. I'm so stupid for coming here. What am I doing? She looks completely, angelically stunning.* He realized he stared at her for far too long.

Kentwood turned to leave, and Franny spouted out without hesitation, "Please do come in. We can speak in the library. It is by far the warmest room in the house. Cecilia has the night off. She takes one night off every week to stay with her sister in the village." *Oh, for mercy's sake, I'm blabbering.* "Fear not, I am on the shelf and not seeking to marry. That ship sailed off long ago." *I sound completely desperate. Stupid. Stupid. Stupid. Do just shut up.* Franny ended her embarrassing glib, "I would love the company. Please, do stay." *Oh yes, now I'm begging. Good grief.*

Kentwood looked into Franny eyes and recognized they sparked an amber hue. Her eyes were fascinating at the way the colors change with whatever lighting was bestowed upon her beautiful face. He was falling under her spell again. He slightly shook his head to bring him back down to earth. Stepping into the foyer, he almost lost control of his manners and kissed her right there and then. Franny interrupted the tempting thought, "This way to the library, Your Grace." She closed the door and walked behind him.

"Drink?" Franny offered with trembling hands.

"Yes. That would be most pleasant," Kentwood somberly responded.

"I was enjoying a spot of wine. Will that suffice?"

"Wine sounds lovely. Thank you."

Apprehensive on how to approach the situation, Franny silently handed the glass to Kentwood. As he took the drink from Franny, his fingers lightly touched her. The brush of her fingers sent a shiver of want through his body. *Hell, and damnation!* He wanted to make Franny his. The beseeching lust between them was mystical.

The touch of Kentwood's fingers immediately produced an uneasiness between Franny's legs – a sort of tingle. She felt like another log was put on the fire. The heat in the room increased by many degrees, her cheeks blushed, and she became lightheaded. *Bloody hell.*

Taking the glass to his lips, Kentwood let the smoothness of the wine linger in his mouth for a bit before swallowing. "I come here tonight to offer an explanation for my poor behavior today. It is now my turn to apologize." He raised his head and eyed Franny.

Franny took a pause before reacting as she was shocked to hear his unnecessary omission. "There is no need for apologies, Your Grace. Obviously, you are experiencing some kind of distress."

"Cease." Kentwood put his hand up in the air in a most ducal manner. "I must do this. I need to explain. Please allow me."

At least he was displaying some type of fervor. Unlike before at dinner, Franny thought.

Standing by the fire he relinquished his tale, starting with his dear brother, John. It was a hotter summer than most in the past. Both boys wanted to cool off in their favorite swimming pond on the estate, Bayberry Hall, the same residence that Kentwood was repairing and that was adjacent to Audrey Manor. Kentwood explained how the hot summer and below average rain caused the pond's bottom vegetation to grow thick and tall. John went underwater and never came back up. He was tangled in the weeds below the surface. Kentwood noted how he tried in vain to save John. He was able to retrieve his body and bring it to the grassy area beside the water. His cries sent the groundskeepers and his father running. When his father came upon the scene, he immediately blamed Kentwood.

Franny reached out and brushed Kentwood's arm to soothe him. As tears welled in his eyes, Kentwood stared off into the distance and said, "John was the heir and my father's favorite. The only way he knew to grieve John's death was by blaming me."

Kentwood continued to disclose how the beatings began immediately. His father believed Kentwood must pay for his brother's death. He told Franny everything. His mother noticed the beatings and urged his father to send Kentwood away for his schooling. She convinced her husband to do so, and Kentwood escaped to Eton, never to came back home. Instead, he spent his time off from school with the family of the Earl of Warwick. His mother fell into a deep sadness and never recovered. She died while he was at school when he was fourteen. His father never returned to Bayberry, hence the need for so many necessary repairs.

"So, I've committed my efforts to bring Bayberry Hall back to glory and make it my main residence. Both my brother and mother are buried there, and I wish to be near them. My father is buried elsewhere and resting in hell." Kentwood drank the rest of his wine in one gulp and asked, "Do you have something stronger, perhaps?"

"Your Grace, I'm very sorry for your loss and pain. My heart breaks for you and I wish I could make it disappear. Talking about it is a step in the right direction. I will always lend an ear to listen whenever you need."

"Thank you, Miss Lane. Perhaps you are right. I do feel a little peace sharing the story." He turned to Franny and looked baffled, he continued, "I've never shared my past with anyone. You have a most confounding power over me."

Putting his empty goblet on the mantle, he stepped closer to Franny. He noticed her naked feet. *She has the most delectable toes.*

"I purpose we start over. I'll go first. I am Lord Bennett David Wheeler, the Duke of Kentwood." With a bow and devilish grin, he continued, "Some call me the Adorable Duke." He flashed a silly smile, pointing to his face. "I think because of these dimples." He paused and continued, "I had a wonderful childhood until my brother died, a devasting adolescence at the hands of my father, and thus far a rather lonely adulthood while trying to figure out how to run all the ducal properties with prosperous efficiency."

Smiling and welcoming the positive conversation, Franny said, "Your Grace, I am Miss Francesca Maria Lane. According to English law, I am a bastard, *definitely not* a lady. My mother was half-Italian and my father a duke. Along with my half-brothers, we manage thirteen estates, a shipping business, and with the help of my mother's family, an olive grove in Italy. I am on the shelf at seven and twenty. I believe women can do anything as good as a man can do. It is a pleasure to make your acquaintance." She then curtsied in a flirtatious fashion, never letting her eyes leave his.

Kentwood, acting like a true rake with a seductive grin, came to Franny's side and put his arm around her front waistline area. They looked at each other side-by-side at the shoulder line. She was slightly looking up at him and he was slightly looking down at her – staring at one another trying to figure out what the other was thinking. Kentwood questioned, "A bluestocking, are you?"

"Oh, my stockings are very white. I assure you. Very pure indeed," Franny flirtatiously replied while lifting her nose a tad higher. Perhaps the wine caused her to be a bit braver and bolder. She was hypnotized by his beauty. The room seemed to be getting smaller. Her breathing increased, causing her breasts to lift higher with her inhales and then lower with her exhales. Her lips slightly parted. She was under his control.

He leaned down and brushed his cheek against hers and whispered in her ear, "Pure you say. Perhaps we can remedy that." Franny's scent of lemon and lavender monopolized his wits, intoxicating him.

Franny leaned into his cheek more with the side of her face. Feather-like, she rubbed back and forth against his skin. It was all too much. With the softest tone of voice she said, "Your Grace, this...."

Kentwood interrupted, "Bennett. Please call me Bennett."

In a teasing matter, Franny said with a mischievous smile, "And you can call me Miss Lane."

Bennett brought his arm around to her back, swirled her to face him directly, then took his hand to her cheek and softly touched her. "I must leave." Putting his forehead down to hers, he continued, "Whatever this is between us, it consumes me, and I fear I will ravish you. I want you. I want to kiss you. You have entrapped me. You terrify me and excite me at the same time. I don't know if you will bring my heart the greatest of happiness or destroy it." With his hand he gently lifted her chin up so their eyes met. Shaking his head and letting out a frustrated sigh, "I must leave. I look forward to my education tomorrow regarding the irrigation project. Goodnight, Miss Lane."

As Kentwood started to walk away, Franny grabbed his hand and intertwined their fingers together. She needed him. She wanted him. The force between them was more than lust. She didn't want to lose it. His hand in hers was soft and downy like. Throwing all caution into the wind, Franny believed this was the only moment in her life to ever feel this way. She wanted to intake how much more she could experience, and she wanted Bennett to be the man to help her. Ruination be damned. She was never to marry, and she believed Kentwood would give her the greatest pleasure she could ever experience. *Why deprive myself of the touch of a man? Especially when it feels so right with him.*

Franny whispered, "Bennett... stay."

He turned to her, still holding her hand, and declared, "If I stay, I will kiss you. If I kiss you, I will not be leaving. I want to make that very clear. I will not be leaving. I want you more than anything I've ever wanted in my whole life. I can't explain it. I need you...."

Before he could finish his declaration, Franny forcefully pressed her lips on his. She mustered every ounce of passion and wanton into that kiss, and he reciprocated in kind. At that very moment, nothing else mattered.

Bennett wrapped his arm around her waist and pulled her into his body. Franny raised her hands up – one hand gripping his shoulder with all her might to steady herself and the other hand moving up the back of his nape, weaving into his hair. Even though their bodies pressed against each other as hard as they could be, it wasn't enough. Franny needed to be closer. His hair between her fingers was her undoing. It felt like silk, and she wanted to discover what the rest of his body felt like. She wanted to feel all of him – explore his body. She needed to feel his skin – to touch every part of him.

Bennett grabbed her face and continued his onslaught of kisses. Their tongues waltzed perfectly together, tasting the bouquet of remnants from the wine. Their lips produced a feverish intensity that just kept building momentum. Franny stopped the frolic and put her forehead on his chin. She stepped back from him. Her hair framed her torso and face, Bennett swore he was standing in front of a goddess. With no words spoken, Franny took Bennett's hand and led him up the grand staircase to her chamber. She seductively looked back at him as they ascended. He was bewitched, in a trance, as she led the way upstairs.

In her chamber, she took a step back and turned to Bennett. Slowly, she started to undress. First, she untied her covering. He stepped to her and slowly took his hands and brushed lightly across her clavicle. He moved his hands from her shoulders to the outside of her arms causing the robe to fall to the floor. Bennett raised Franny's arms and slowly lifted her chemise over her head, unlocking the beauty of her body little by little. First her thighs, then her midsection, then her delightful breasts. It was like unwrapping a present.

Bennett gently swept her hair behind her back and kissed her neck. He brushed his face by her cheek and breathlessly said, "My God, you are beautiful."

Bennett gave a feather-like kiss to Franny's forehead. Then he brought his lips down to hers. This time the kisses were filled with so much more than simple lust. The kisses started slowly, very delicately with more emotion, and then turned into something deeper – something more sensual. Franny couldn't find a word to describe it. The atmosphere of the room led her to believe that there was no one else in the world except for her and Bennett. Just the two of them and the powerful force that fused them together.

While frantically kissing, Franny reached and pulled his coat off. She pulled his shirt out from his breeches and Bennett helped to lift it over his head, revealing his skin. Franny stopped kissing and took a deep breath. With shaking fingers, she placed them on his hard chest. It was smooth, bare, and chiseled by God. She ran her hands down his pectorals to his rippled abdomen. Then grabbed the buttons of his pants and looked up to Bennett and said, "You are magnificent."

Bennett lifted her up and sat her on the edge of the large four poster oak bed. He went down to his knees and pulled Franny's undergarments off. Sitting on the side of the bed with her legs hanging off the edge, Bennett came up to her and kissed her again with immense affection. Franny didn't care that she was completely naked. Right at that time and place it felt like the most natural thing to be – to be with Bennett. She felt safe. She felt wanted. She needed more.

Bennett gently laid her back on top of the bed and worked his sinful, lush lips down her neck to her breast. He took her nipple into his mouth and flicked it with his tongue. Franny moaned with pleasure, her back slightly arched at the sensation and she started to caress his hair. After he was done with that nipple, he slid over to the other one. The act made Franny ache with need between her legs. She needed to be touched where she would touch herself in the privacy of her chamber. Just as the need was reaching a climax, Bennett went back down on his knees at the side of the bed and kissed down her stomach to the curls of her womanhood. He lifted both of her long legs over his broad shoulders and pulled her closer to the edge of bed, so her bottom was almost falling off.

"Bennett?" Franny questioned what he was doing.

"Shhh. Allow me to worship you," he said in a reassuring whisper. He then parted her slit with his fingers and took his tongue to her clit, sliding his tongue back and forth across the sensitive flesh.

Jesus, Joseph, and Mary. Franny let out a short cry, grabbed his head and pushed him harder against her. She was experiencing pure ecstasy. As Bennett kept the onslaught of his tongue going, he took one hand and reached for her breast. With his thumb, he made small circular movements at the very tip of her nipple. The other hand went to her sex, and he slid a finger deep inside her, going in and out of her at a slow, torturing pace. All the while, his tongue kept lapping at her nubbin. Franny came undone. Her whole body shivered with bliss sending her to a different world. She let out a cry when she reached her apex and yelped his name, "Oh, Bennett."

Bennett took a few moments to allow Franny to come back down from her zenith. He lightly kissed the inside of her thighs, her knees, all the way to her ankles. Bennett stood and gently lifted her to be completely on the bed. Franny laid her head into his chest. Her entire body was limp from the pleasurable encounter. Bennett took his breeches off. Franny was spellbound by the sight of his shaft. She inquisitively asked, "Can I touch you?"

Without waiting for permission, Franny gently took her fingers and rubbed his tip. She was amazed at how soft it felt. Then she took her finger and allowed it to travel down his length.

Bennett grabbed her hand and brought it to his lips. "I want you. I need you."

He climbed on top of her, leaning his body on both his elbows as he rested between her parted legs. He brushed her hair away from her face and lovingly looked into her eyes. The back of his hand brushed the side of Franny's cheek as she leaned into it. He lifted her hips slightly and placed Little Buddy at her entrance. Breathing deeply, Bennett asked, "Do you want me to stop?"

"No." Franny grabbed his face and reassured Bennett, "I have never wanted anything more."

Bennett placed his forehead on hers, trying to control himself. Franny placed her hands on his hips and urged him to continue. Picking up on her cue, Bennett stared into Franny's eyes and forcefully pushed forward, plunging inside her. Franny inhaled the pain with a moan, grabbed his shoulders, and dug her nails into him. Bennett moaned. To ease her discomfort, he kissed her with a wrath of devotion. He started to pull slightly out and then back in. Very slowly. Very affectionately. Out and in.

Franny would never regret this moment – his body becoming one with hers. She may never wed. She may never understand what love is between a husband and wife, but she had this very moment with Bennett, and it was perfect. He was perfect. Franny began to relax, and her hips started to sway with him – as if they danced on water creating their own waves. Their bodies molded perfectly together. Bennett nestled his head against hers as he increased the pace of the rhythmic frolic. He wanted to make this so good for her.

Bennett had been with other women, but it was always just for the pleasure of being pleasured. With Franny, it was more. He couldn't explain it, but he knew it was rare. The passion and actual physical feeling were more than he ever thought possible. It was as if time just stood still. He wanted to kiss every part of her. He was falling in love with her. There was no other explanation. After what they shared, he couldn't be with anyone else. She ruined him for any women that may follow.

Bennett grabbed Franny's hand, weaving their fingers together and pulled it over her head. Franny started to feel her body come to another wave of euphoria. She raised her long legs over his lower back and locked them together, trying to hold him as close to her body as she could. With a surprised grin, Bennett slightly raised up onto his elbow to admire her. Both looked at each other in pure amazement at what was happening. Wondering what this was all about and yet not wanting it to never ever end. Franny grabbed his face and lightly stroked his cheek. They stared at each other in awe as they climaxed together.

A tear fell from Franny's face. Bennett tenderly wiped it away. He rolled to his back, grabbed the blanket laying at the edge of the bed and covered them. He brought Franny's head to rest on his chest. No words spoken. He kissed the top of her crown and calmly brushed her hair while holding her. He didn't want to leave. She never felt so at home than in his arms. *Home.* The idea of having a home and family of her own was just a dream for Franny. Dare she hope it could be a reality?

Bennett started imagining what a future with Miss Lane might be like – how beautiful their children would be. His heart skipped a beat and he realized he was going to make her his Duchess. Franny closed her eyes and savored the moment before she drifted to sleep, snuggled safely in the warmth of Bennett's arms.

Chapter Seven

"Good morning milady. The sun, she is a shining today!" Cecilia shouted as she burst into Franny's bedchamber. "What shall we be wearing today? Perhaps a purple hue? Or perhaps you want to bathe first? Yes, I do believe you *need* to bathe."

Cecilia was no daft woman. She knew exactly what events occurred during her absence. Part of her was furious that Franny would allow such liberties, yet the other part of her was happy for Franny. She recalled her own memories with her husband during the days of their courtship - how she and Ronnie laid together in the hay loft of her father's barn. *"Ahh, young love,"* she thought to herself.

"I think I will start the day off with a ride. One must take advantage of the weather. As you said the sun is shining. Most definitely a bath afterwards. Then I must meet up with Edward and Kentwood to go over business details."

Franny tried not to smile too much. She squinted her eyes when Cecilia pulled the drapery back as the lightness of the day filtrated the room. By the way Cecilia was acting, Franny knew she suspected something happened last night. The dear woman was practically having another case of the so-called vapors.

"I noticed two empty goblets on the fireplace mantle of the library. May I inquire if perhaps Lord Millington stopped by for a nightcap or maybe Lord Miles?" The mystery of it all was eating up the insides of Cecilia. She had to know if it was indeed the Duke of Kentwood that shared a drink with her dearest Franny.

"As a matter of fact, it was the Duke of Kentwood." Franny would not hide the truth from Cecilia. She knew all the secrets of Franny's life.

"And are we friends now?" Cecilia asked as she picked up Franny's housecoat from the floor.

Still laying in her bed with the covers over her, Franny turned her gaze to the window and soaked in the sunshine beaming into the room. Remembering all that occurred between her and Kentwood, Franny smiled, bit her lower lip, and said, "Oh, yes, we are most indeed friends. I shall start educating him on how we manage the ducal assets and the shipping company. He hopes he can turn his dilapidated properties into more prosperous ones."

Franny rolled onto her stomach, still not believing that last night happened. *Pray tell, it wasn't a dream.* She placed her hand under the pillow. She was surprised to find a note. Propped up on her elbows she read the missive:

You are a marvelous wonder.

With all my love,

B

Love?

He ended the sweet note with the word, love. Elation and horror swept through Franny. She did not regret last night. She wished he was still in bed with her. Her feelings for him were… well… she was not sure. She lusted for him but love? *Is this love? No. It is too soon. One does not instantly fall in love. I am supposed to loathe him. Lust and infatuation are what happened last night. It must be this way.*

"Is that some kind of correspondence so early in the morning? Are you working on poetry at night when I'm gone?" Cecilia was not going to let this rest. She stood in the middle of the room with her hands on her hips and continued nagging, "I'm sorry milady. I am going to speak out of line. It is only because I care deeply for you. I gather you and the Duke did things that 'just friends' don't do. Part of me is thrilled for you. The motherly side of me must advise that you proceed with caution. Protect your heart and perhaps take insurances so there are no consequences *born*."

Franny giggled and threw the covers back. "Oh Cecilia, rest assured, I will proceed with the topmost discretion. I value the kindred affinity you and I have. Thank you for caring the way you do." Franny was satisfied she wasn't lying to Cecilia. Besides, at twenty-seven years old, what was the point? She was a grown, independent woman with means and more freedom than most married women.

Cecilia sat on the edge of the bed and gave Franny a scowling face. With a very concerned tone, she gave a warning, "A duke is one of the highest echelon of stations. Marriage to his lot is not to be expected from a woman of your rank. Pray forgive me. Be protective of your heart. A mistress is all he will have from you."

Cecilia was correct. That was the reality of the situation. Franny reached for Cecilia's hand and squeezed it, trying not to show her disappointment. "Relax by friend, I will protect my heart. At my age, one must take advantage of once in a lifetime opportunities." Franny winked at Cecilia. "Oh! I almost forgot. Kentwood's cousin and ward, Lady Sophia, is expected to arrive today. I shall be staying at the main house as her companion and at times chaperone. I do believe her stay is for a fortnight. You are welcome to stay here or the main house, your choice."

Cecilia pondered the question. She started to fold the clothes she gathered when she held up a man's sock. Dangling the sock in the air, she sarcastically said, "Just friends?" She placed the folded clothing at the end of the bed and continued, "Daresay, how old is Lady Sophia?"

Embarrassed, Franny said, "That would be Bennett's sock. Poor foot must be cold this morning." Franny put her knuckles into her mouth to keep the giggles at bay. "As for Lady Sophia's age, I believe her to be twenty, and if I recall from the gossip rags, she was a diamond of her first season."

"Thank you for the clarification of *all* my questions, milady." Cecilia shook her head and declared, "I shall stay at the main house to be close to you – just in case you may have need of me. If this visitor proves to be even remotely vivacious and pretty as your sources say, you will need additional reinforcements in monitoring your brothers, especially Lord Miles. Now, let's get you out of here and on your morning ride before you break your fast. You have a busy day it seems."

Wearing men's breeches underneath her navy riding skirt with black riding boots, Franny had her hair in a long braid, topped with a veiled, navy riding hat. She wore a white button-down ruffled corset covered with a gold embellished tailed navy jacket. Blake was at the stables when she entered to say good morning to her beloved horse, Mouse. "Good morning, Miss Lane. If I may say, you look rather ravishing this morning." He winked at Franny as he saddled Mouse for her ride.

Did he know? Can he tell I was deflowered last night? Does my body scream out, "I'm no longer a virgin!" Perhaps a servant saw something and now spreads gossip? Bloody hell! I need to get a grip on my inner thoughts.

Franny decided to fire back, and in a very joking voice said, "Blake, are you attempting to flirt with my person? I daresay a scandal will now ensue." She winked back at him.

Blake let out a big laugh that came from deep inside one's stomach. "Miss Lane, you never cease to surprise me."

"By chance has the Duke of Kentwood gone for a ride this morning?" Franny had to inquire.

"Indeed, he did. Already returned. He was extremely chipper. His smile and dimples never dimmed. No wonder they call him the Adorable Duke," Blake replied with a mischievous grin.

Franny blushed.

Blake helped Franny ascend onto Mouse. Her ungloved hand reached for Blake's hand as he assisted her into the saddle. Franny noticed when their hands touched that it didn't feel the same as when she touched Bennett's hands. Bennett's touch sent a commanding charge through her body that engulfed her whole person. *Blast! I will not be his mistress. My heart is doomed.*

"Are you alright milady?" Blake asked with a puzzled look and concerned voice, probably because Franny was still holding his hand.

"Yes, pardon… uhm… just a moment of woolgathering. My apologies." Franny shook her head and took off in an immediate gallop. She had never been this confused and disoriented. The ride will help her trudge through the many thoughts flying around in her mind.

Kentwood entered the morning room of Audrey Manor and helped himself to the side table that hosted the breakfast spread. Millington was already at the table having coffee and reading the latest news sheets. He asked, "How was your sleep, Kentwood? I didn't see you in the evening for a nightcap." Millington looked like he was about to interrogate the latest round up of possible French spies. His face was one that would win many games of whist since it never gave an indication of what cards he held in his hand.

"Good morning, Millington. If you recall, I had a bit of a headache at dinner. Took to my chamber all night. I must have needed some good sleep because I feel quite rejuvenated this morning." Kentwood pleasantly smiled as he replied to Millington. He seated himself directly across from his lover's brother. Kentwood recalled last evening with Miss Lane. He wished he was able to stay in her bed all night. He wanted to see what she looked like when the sun's first rays trickled upon her body in the morning – what color her eyes would be. He was longing to wake up with her wrapped in his arms. His body ached to be next to her again.

"Deep in thought man? You were up at the crack of dawn. My valet said you went riding. Was it muddy out by the stables this morn? One of the footmen complained of wiping up muddy boot prints. Perhaps it was Miles. He is always running about with no cares in the world for propriety." Millington seemed to be implying that Kentwood was out all night and guilty of the messed flooring.

Feeling quite uneasy, Kentwood recalled how stupid it was for him to enter the house last night through the front foyer. He directed back, "Millington, with your firing of questions, one may suspect you work for the Home Office." Kentwood was perplexed and thought to himself, "*Drat and Damnation! Does he know his beloved sister and I were together last night? Did a servant see me leave? I was so careful. I must not let this fill me with paranoia. He's just making small talk.*" Kentwood continued the conversation with Millington, "The stable area was a bit soggy this morning from the night's frost. I came back in through the servants' quarters to drop off my Hessians for cleaning. I hope I am not overstepping my stay by doing that." Kentwood wasn't lying. He did come back into the house through the servants' quarters after his morning ride.

With the news sheet up in front of his face, Millington dropped it just enough to show his eyes glaring at Kentwood and nonchalantly said, "Not a problem at all, *old chap*. I only inquired since I do not like having the staff do extra work because of the carelessness with one's boots."

Blazes! Millington suspected something untoward happened last night. Kentwood's paranoia increased tenfold. Kentwood was finishing his tasty breakfast of sausage, eggs, and toast when Lord Miles entered the room.

"Good, glorious morning dear brother! And Kentwood! How goes your morning old chap?" Always so damn chipper, Miles grabbed some nourishment and summoned for some coffee. He then took the chair to Kentwood's left and moved it even closer to Kentwood. Upon sitting down, Miles grabbed Kentwood's shoulder with a grip so forceful that he hit the nerve under Kentwood's shoulder blade sending a sharp pain down Kentwood's arm.

Fuck, they know. Kentwood did not flinch. He didn't want the brothers to see how uncomfortable he truly was. Miles leaned closer to Kentwood's ear and grabbed the top of his thigh hard enough to instigate an immediate cramp. In a voice that knew the truth of last night, Miles asked, "Do tell me dearest fossil, how was your evening? Did you find a remedy for your megrim?"

Miles snapped his fingers with authority at the footmen, causing all the servants to leave the room at once, closing the doors. Kentwood was gravely concerned for his being. Trapped like a treed fox by the dogs he was. Most unsettled, Kentwood dared not look at either of the brothers. He pursed his lips together and with a most annoyed voice said, "As I told your brother just a moment ago, I took to my bed all night. Just needed some sleep. I feel very well today. Thank you for inquiring."

Miles turned to Kentwood and said in a threatening, questionable voice, "Are you *most positive* you were in your *own* bed last night?"

Kentwood very abruptly stood up, knocking the chair over. He threw his napkin on the table. Glaring down on Miles and with an authoritative voice said, "If you have something to say, man, please say it. Out with it!"

Millington put the news sheet down, dappled the corners of his mouth with his napkin and calmly spoke, "*Tsk. Tsk.* Kentwood, please do repair your chair to its proper place and sit." Millington made a gesture with his arm, his palm open to the sky implying Kentwood to make haste and be seated.

Miles mocked Kentwood, "Well... well, look at the Adorable Duke now. Looking more like quite the foozler."

Kentwood did as directed and sat back down. He knew he couldn't take both brothers on at the same time. They were the same size as him, but a bit meatier, stronger and a decade younger.

Bloody Hell.

Miles shamed Kentwood by patting him on the head like he was a loyal dog and said, "Good boy."

"Miles that will be enough," Millington chimed in, still the model of tranquility. "Let's talk as gentlemen and discuss the business of you *bedding* my sister." Millington was speaking with his teeth closed in a malign fashion.

Kentwood was sure he was going to die a slow death. There was little doubt about it. One fist at a time into his skull. The look on Millington's face just now was of pure disgust and rage. Obviously, the brothers planned this well-thought-out assassination.

How am I going to get out of this? The two brothers remind me of John and myself.

All Kentwood could think of was *"the truth shall set you free"* from the scriptures of John in the Gospels. If ever there was evidence for guardian angels, this was one of those moments. His beloved, departed brother, John, conveniently appeared in his mind with tidbits from the past when the need arose. It happened time and time again when Kentwood needed a supporting voice. *The truth shall set you free* was one of John's favorite things to say. That was it. The truth.

Kentwood's heart was being filled with wisdom from his brother. He recalled last evening's magical experience with Miss Lane. He almost chuckled out loud at the thought of how the woman could bring him so much vexation, passion, and wonderment at the same time. The combination of it all produced a small, peaceful smile on his face. *What is this emotion I feel for Miss Lane?* In his mind, Kentwood quickly ran an inventory of his feelings for Miss Lane:

The want to be with her at all times.

The want to protect her.

The want to make love to her.

The want to be her friend.

The want to live the rest of my days with her.

The want to make love to her. Oh wait, already said that one.

The want to make her happy.

CRACK!

"Bloody hell! What in the deuce?! Why did you hit me?!" Kentwood started rubbing his cheek for comfort.

"I had to wipe that smirk off your bloody, adorable face. How dare you reminisce about your tryst with my sister right in front of us! Count your blessings I'm still not pounding your skull and then using your hair to mop up the mess." Miles looked a bit crazed. "*Ha!* Oh, that felt good. Perhaps just one more time."

CRACK!

Miles let out a ludicrous laugh. He surprised himself with how he found it quite exhilarating defending Franny's honor and hitting the Adorable Duke's face.

Kentwood's rubbed down his cheek and exclaimed, "I love her!" Kentwood had no control over his thoughts. No filter was on to stop his proclamation. He loved Franny with the protective fierceness of a Viking warrior. He loved her more than his own life. The thought of losing her sent a wave of desperation through his body. She was beautiful, witty, daring, and intelligent. He was in love with Miss Lane, and he wasn't going to let her mollycoddling brothers destroy a future with her.

"I. Love. Her."

"You what?" Both Miles and Millington shouted back in disbelief.

"I love her. I accept it seems very unlikely given our cold beginning, but I can't denounce it. I love her. I thought it was just lust because she is undeniably beautiful, but it is so much more. I can't explain it. So much passion is between us."

"Cease!" Edward yelled with a hand up in a halting matter. "I don't want to hear E-V-E-R-Y-T-H-I-N-G. Bloody hell, what is wrong with you?"

Miles sat down in shock with his hand going through his hair and eyebrows raised up. In a surprised voice that almost squeaked he exclaimed, "Holy fuck! I wasn't expecting that response. Capital!"

Wearily, with hands rubbing down his face, Millington delicately asked, "And does she return your affections?" Millington knew his sister well. He knew she had much animosity toward Kentwood's family. He recognized the stubbornness and strong-willed mind of Franny. Millington feared Kentwood's heart would be destroyed, not so much his sister's.

Looking defeated, Kentwood sadly answered, "I am not certain."

"Well, we are the only persons that are aware of this event, and nothing needs to be done in haste," Millington advised.

"Marriage is the only option. I fear I was not prepared for last night's events and necessary precautions were null and void during our relations," Kentwood admitted. He then braced his body for what would occur next.

CRACK!

Miles landed a blow to Kentwood's ribs. Miles stood up and paced back and forth behind where Kentwood was seated at the table.

"What the fucking fuck?! You imbecile. Everyone man of the peerage knows you pump, and then you dump. What were you thinking?" He shook his head in disaccord and said, "Never mind, I do not what to know."

Millington, showing no emotion, said, "Kentwood, you are at sixes and sevens. Your rank indicates you need to marry a woman of the same station. Franny is not that. You will produce a scandal no matter what you do. Are you prepared for that?"

Kentwood was in a pickling predicament. He loved Franny but to marry her would cause scandal just because of who she is – a bastard, half-blood exotic. That would not do well for his position in the House of Lords, yet he can't live without her. Perhaps he could protector her as his mistress. She could be with child, but it's too early to fathom that. Perhaps the notion of waiting to see if the union produced a babe was the best solution at this time, especially since he did not know of Miss Lane's feelings for him. Kentwood offered an elucidation, "I suppose for now, we will wait and see if the union produced an issue. Millington, as you said, we do not need to make a hasty decision straight away."

Still pacing back and forth behind Kentwood, Miles declared, "And if an issue comes about, what then? And don't say you will protect her as your mistress?"

Just then the butler, Mr. Grizwold, knocked and entered the room. Otherwise known as Griz, the butler had been with the family since Millington and Miles were babes. With salt and pepper hair, his stature was short but still very strong, even at the age of two and fifty. Just like Cecilia, the family held Griz in high regard and treated him more like a family member rather than a servant. Griz bowed and announced, "Carriage approaching, Your Grace."

"That will be my ward, Lady Sophia," announced Kentwood.

"This conversation is not over, Kentwood," Millington stressed.

All three men arose from their seats and headed to the door in order to greet the arriving Lady Sophia on the front lawn. On the way out of the morning room Millington lightly patted Kentwood's shoulder, and with a more sympathetic voice spoke, "We will discuss this later. My sister is at her majority and independent. She makes her own decisions. I do not agree with whatever happened between you two last night. However right now, let's go welcome your cousin."

Chapter Eight

Millington, Kentwood, Lord Miles and Griz positioned themselves along the gravel pathway before the front lawn. The black carriage being pulled by a team of gorgeous reddish-brown Cleveland Bays lurched along the drive. The branches of the silver birch trees that lined the entrance to Audrey Manor were starting to bud. Soon their brilliant leaves would dun baubles of sparkling jewels that twinkled in the sunlight. The carriage rolled to a stop in front of the men. A footman put a wooden step at the carriage door and opened it. A most delicate, petite, white-laced gloved hand emerged. As soon as Miles saw the hand, he jumped in front of the footman and offered his assistance.

Lady Sophia exited the carriage wearing a light pink, black trimmed travel suit and matching bonnet. Her light blond hair in a simple chiffon had a few longer curls dangled on the sides of her head. She had a porcelain skin with a sprinkle of freckles that graced her button nose. She grabbed the hand presented to her and paused, realizing it was not a servant nor her cousin. Looking at Miles she noticed how insanely handsome he was. She stopped breathing. His touch seared through her skin right down to her core and left her wanting for more.

When he saw her eyes, Miles was at that moment forever at the beckon call of Lady Sophia Angelica Wheeler. Her marine blue eyes cast a spell on him. They reminded him of his time in Italy - the warm waters of the Mediterranean. His whole body felt on fire. Leading her down the step, Miles held her hand and said, "Lord Miles at your service, my lady." He kissed the top of her elegantly gloved hand, devilishly stared into her eyes said, "Never before have I believed in love at first sight, but I truly do now."

"Well, my, my, my… Lord Miles, you are surely a most appetizing surprise," Lady Sophia said as she covered her heart with her palm.

Minx. Miles was instantly besotted.

Watching the rather inappropriate events unfold before his eyes, Kentwood leaned to Millington and whispered, "Millington, I see your brother is taking his duty of the reckless spare rather seriously. So, help me, if your brother ruins my cousin, I will have to call for a duel."

"Kentwood, if my brother ruins your cousin, I will be your second. Not his." Millington was shocked that his brother could put on such a display of incorrigible manners.

With a strut of authority, Kentwood interrupted the young couple's tête-à-tête. "Lady Sophia, you look well. I hope the journey wasn't too overtaxing."

Giving a slight curtsy Sophia replied, "Bennett, always the most handsome duke around. I have missed your company."

Coughing into his hand, Millington chimed in, "I am a duke as well and daresay better looking than this old dog." Millington greeted Lady Sophia with a bow and continued, "Lady Sophia, welcome to Audrey Manor. I am Lord Edward Lane, the Duke of Millington. We hope you find your stay a pleasant one."

Sophia glanced between the two brothers and noticed how much their bodies were the same. Hard, tall, and gorgeous. Then she glanced at Kentwood who was at least ten years their senior but nevertheless still very athletic and handsome. "Thank you, Your Grace. Oh dear, being surrounded by you three impressive specimens could lead a lady to swoon," Lady Sophia said with a flirtatious smile as she waved her fan in front of her chest.

Millington let out a sigh. First, he had to deal with the revelation of Kentwood bedding his sister, and now he looked between his brother and Lady Sophia, all he could think of was how to avoid the scandal of Miles debauching Kentwood's ward. Being a young duke was complicated. As head of the family, he was responsible for his family's wellbeing and reputation, but as a young man, he wanted his fun as well. "*Perhaps someday I will have a reckless romp in the hay with a woman of my choosing*," he thought. But today was not that day.

"Come. You must be tired from your travels. Griz, please see that Lady Sophia's things are brought to the Meadow Suite," directed Millington as he led everyone to enter the house.

In the entry foyer, footmen scrambled to take everyone's coats, gloves, and hats. The main door opened, announcing the arrival of Franny and her maid, Cecilia. As soon as Franny entered, her eyes immediately cast onto Kentwood. His gaze directed the same attention right back to her. Her mouth slightly opened as she caught her breath. He looked so heavenly. He was almost entirely dressed in black, all but his shirt, which was white with a black vest over it. The dark colors enhanced his dreaming eyes of chocolate and darkened his eyelashes even more. She noticed the side of his face was bright red – like he had a rash or had been hit by something. Then she noticed her brothers glared between Kentwood and her. *Oh dear. They know.*

Suspiciously looking back and forth between Franny and Kentwood, Lady Sophia said with a big smile, "Dearest cousin, it appears you are well acquainted with the newly arrived guest."

Miles whispered in Sophia's ear with a seductive tone, "Oh, he knows her very well."

Millington gave Miles a stern gaze, warning him to behave.

Lady Sophia cleared her throat, "As I was saying, please cousin, introduce us. I was fretting that I would be the only female present at Audrey Manor. I'm very relieved to see I am not."

Kentwood grabbed Sophia's hand and pulled her away from Miles and stepped towards Franny and bowed. In a rather dismal voice he said, "Good day, Miss Lane. May I introduce my cousin and ward, Lady Sophia Wheeler. Cousin, this is Miss Francesca Lane. She will be your companion and chaperone during your stay."

"Miss Lane. Pleasure. I have an inkling we will be fast friends," said Sophia as she slightly curtsied.

Franny nervously wondered what events had occurred within the walls of Audrey Manor since last evening, for the tension amongst everyone was stifling. She put on a welcoming smile and said to Sophia, "Lady Sophia. It is an honor to make your acquaintance. I look forward to becoming more acquainted with you. Franny glanced back to Kentwood's face. The once red rash on his cheek changed to a bluish hue.

Miles kept staring at Sophia, to the point that it was deemed inappropriate, and he didn't care. He chimed in, "Lady Sophia, after your rest, may I entertain you with a walk of the grardens? Of course, with a chaperone as well. Perhaps Franny can join us."

Sophia instantly replied with much happiness, "Lord Miles, that is a capital idea. Thank you. That is if it is permissible with you, dearest cousin." She looked to Kentwood for approval.

At this point in his day, Kentwood didn't give a damn about anything. He should care about the way Miles was preying upon his cousin like a hungry owl searching for a sweet mouse to devour, but he was just mentally and emotionally exhausted. Kentwood replied, "As long as Miss Lane doesn't mind accompanying you."

"I do not mind at all. I am happy to tag along and *not* keep my distance from you whatsoever," Franny said with a warning to the two young, potential lovers.

As the welcoming party dissipated, Millington pulled Cecilia and Griz aside. "Griz, please put Franny in the master suite with Lady Sophia in the connecting chamber. I will move to the East Wing where Miles and the Duke of Kentwood are situated. This is unprecedented, but, Cecilia, your duties will be best served by staying in the chamber across from the master suite in the West Wing. The more eyes the better. Dearest Cecilia, I do believe you understand my actions for this."

"I do, Your Grace. Very wise decision indeed," Cecilia said nodding her head in agreement.

"With whatever occurred between my sister and Kentwood, and now Miles facetiously declaring his undying love for Lady Sophia, we must be vigilant so no scandal will come from this impromptu house party."

"Bennett, we need to talk." Franny walked to Kentwood's side. He was heading to his chamber. She grabbed his hand and jolted him into the library, closing the door. She paced along the oak floor in front of the bookcases. "Bennett, we need to talk about last night."

"Was it not satisfactory for you?" He gave Franny a wicked smile. Bennett couldn't help himself. He had been waiting all morning to see her again.

Coming to an abrupt stop with a slight growl escaping her, Franny responded, "That is most arrogant of you to ask. Yet, that is the problem. It was. It was very, very satisfactory. To the point that I wish for more. And by the way, you should rename Little Buddy, he is not so little." She waved her hand at Kentwood's midsection. Franny paced the floor again and asked, "What happened to your face?"

Bennett stood by the door with his hands behind his back wondering why Franny seemed so upset and responded, "They know."

Franny stopped pacing, looked right at Bennett and with a distressed tone asked, "Miles and Edward?"

"Yes. Breakfast was most enjoyable," Bennett said sarcastically.

Franny, tried not to look affected by the news and said, "Oh, it means nothing that they ascertained our bedding. I am an independent woman. Please understand you have no obligations to me because of last night's shenanigans."

Shenanigans? Was that all it was to her? Kentwood was devastated. He refused to be downtrodden and spoke, "Millington said the same about your independent spirit, but he is not happy. Your brother should work for the Home Office. He's bloody good at interrogating."

"He does work for the Home Office. We help with relations between the Crown and Italy. I believe he is quite privy to the events of Napoleon and his cronies." Franny continued and further explained how the family's shipping company smuggled goods into France to help arm those that fought against Napoleon. Franny decided to get back on the subject at hand and asked Kentwood, "Do tell, what can possibly become of this? You and me?"

"I… I do not know," responded Bennett, shaking his head in confusion. He was terrified to make his true feeling for Miss Lane known since it appeared she did not reciprocate them.

Immediately, Franny jumped to conclusions and spoke with an irritated voice, "You don't know?" Franny was irked.

"Listen, I have been with women before you and don't take offense to that, it's just fact. What I can tell you is that last night… I've never experienced anything so powerful before in my life. I don't know what to do now. All I can think of is you. All I want is you. To be with you. To be in you." Kentwood stepped closer to Franny. Close enough that he could smell the scent of her hair - lavender and lemons.

Franny realized she was against his chest and protested, "Let me tell you what I think. I understand completely. I am below you in station and rank and will only serve as a mistress to you. So, listen carefully, Bennett Wheeler, the Adorable Duke of Kentwood, I will not now nor ever be a mistress to you or anyone else. I don't need your coin."

Kentwood grabbed her face with both hands and protested, "No. Not a mistress. For now, can't we just enjoy each other's company?" Bennett wasn't sure what to say and immediately regretted his words. *I am a total clodpoll.*

Franny slapped his hands off her and scolded him, "So, am I to be your whore? Just spread my legs whenever you stop by?"

Letting out a growl of frustration, Kentwood pleaded, "Franny, you are taking this out of context. You could be with child. What happened last night between us was very special, and I daresay, something very few people ever experience. I will never forget it – the passion – it carved a mark on my soul. I am yours."

Kentwood grabbed Franny by the waist. Their cheeks brushed up against each other. Franny closed her eyes trying to fight the mystical force that pulled her closer to him, wanting more. She exhaled a big sigh and stepped back with her hands up in the air in front of her chest. "This can never be - you and me. Our stations are not the same. We will wait to see if I am indeed increasing. That will dictate what we do next. And Kentwood... you are to call me Miss Lane."

Kentwood bellowed an irritated growl as Franny departed the room.

For the next week, Franny avoided Kentwood at all costs.

Chapter Nine

It was a pleasant and sunny afternoon, Edward requested to walk some of the estate with Franny. With her arm wrapped around Edward's, she was soaking up the brilliant sunshine and the unseasonal warmth of the early spring day. Gazing ahead in the distance, Franny spotted Miles and Lady Sophia under the very same tree where she discovered Kentwood's scars – born from the hands of his own father. Her heart once again ached for Kentwood. *What kind of monster would do that to his own flesh and blood? The same kind that destroyed my childhood.* Shaking the thought from her mind, she settled on the sight before her. Miles sat beside Lady Sophia who was holding a blanket around her shoulders. Their conversation produced the sweet smiles of young love.

"What do you make of that?" Edward asked as he witnessed what appeared to be an innocent picnic between two young people. He noticed the frown on Franny's face.

"Miles is easily distracted. He sees a new, bright, shiny object and instantly becomes infatuated with it," Franny answered.

Miles grabbed Sophia's blanket and proceeded to put his arm behind her back and wrapped the blanket around both of them. All snug in a rug like a bug. He positioned the blanket just so, as to protect any unwanted eyes from witnessing him and his picnic guest. Franny suggested to Millington, "Is he stealing a kiss at this moment?"

Edward decided to divulge his observations of Miles and Lady Sophia. "It appears that way. Miles truly seems besotted this time."

Franny, in a sisterly way, punched Millington's arm. "Ugh! I hate that word. Besotted. You use it all the time. Dearest brother, I know your vocabulary to be of a broader range."

Rubbing his arm and acting like he was gravely wounded by Franny's blow, Millington said, "He never leaves her side. Acts like a pathetic little pup. I fear he will cross paths with Kentwood at some point and the ending will result in a duel."

Letting out a sigh, Franny commented, "The only thing we can hope for is discretion among the servants. If we were in town, this would surely turn into the Scandal of the Season."

"Speaking of potential scandals...." Millington thought it was the perfect time to talk about Kentwood.

"Not now Edward," snapped Franny.

"As the Duke of Millington, I am responsible for my family. I do not want to pry into your love life, but I am genuinely concerned about what has developed between you and Kentwood," Millington said as he patted Franny's hand that was hanging on his forearm as they walked.

"I am a grown woman. The decisions I make are mine and mine alone. You hold no responsibility for them." Franny was exhausted about the topic and let out a deep sigh.

"Yes, I am aware of your independent, womanly status. But I must tell you that the man is in misery." Millington was truly worried about Kentwood. The beast was stalking around Audrey Manor in a numbness stupor.

"He is?" Franny's concern was written all over her face. Millington could see she was in love with the man.

Stopping the walk, Millington looked to his sister and said, "Franny, he confessed his love for you."

"He... he did?" Franny was at a loss for words with Millington's testimony.

Millington delicately asked, "Was an offer made?"

"I told him I was not to be his mistress." Franny realized how poorly she handled the situation in the library between her and Kentwood.

Millington responded with a displeased voice, "I see. So, he offered you to be his mistress?"

"No... no, he did not," Franny said. "Please, don't misunderstand the situation."

"Did he offer marriage?" Millington was deuced confused. One thing he had learned from the Kentwood situation and with his wayward, lovesick brother was that he was never going to fall in love.

"No. Well… not exactly. Oh… I do not know. Perhaps he was going to. I may not have handled the situation very well," Franny said while she bit her bottom lip appearing a bit embarrassed by her actions.

"What? You? Not handle a situation well. I am in distress that you would not handle things in a true accord." Millington lightened the mood by teasing his sister. He lightly leaned into her shoulder and grabbed her arm, intertwining his arm with hers and started walking again. "Dearest sister, the Duke of Kentwood is a good man. You cannot hold the sins of his grandfather and his rotten arse of a father against him. He is not like them."

Franny was astonished and said, "You know about…."

Millington interrupted her and said, "Yes, I am aware of the evilness his grandfather did to your mother. I know what his father did to him. Warwick and his family took Kentwood in and practically raised him as one of their own. He never went home once he started at Eton – he didn't even come home for his mother's funeral." Millington took a pause to regain control of his anger and continued, "Kentwood never swam with his shirt off. From what I gathered, Warwick was the one who figured out why and vowed to protect Kentwood after all the facts were uncovered. He was severely, physically abused."

Franny's heart sank. She was at a loss for words and tears started to fall down her cheeks. Millington handed Franny a handkerchief and she dabbed the wetness from her face.

Millington stressed, "I strongly urge you to get to know Kentwood for the man that he is. Do you even know the policies he is pursuing in the House of Lords?"

Looking bewildered Franny answered, "No. I really know little about, His Grace." Franny was coming to the actualization that her stubbornness and closed mindlessness needed to stop. It was preventing her from living a life of happiness. A life that she deserved. Perhaps a life with Kentwood.

Millington educated Franny about the feats Kentwood was trying to perform in Parliament. "He is a champion for abused children, trying in vain to pass laws that protect children from the violent hands of anyone, including their own parents. He is to be applauded for his beliefs but mostly he is up against a brick wall trying to get those notions to become a reality. Hell, even the monarchy has been known to beat their children. But even with all the opposition, Kentwood keeps trying."

"Thank you, Edward. There is much to learn and discover about His Grace. I am such an idiot," Franny said shaking her head.

"Don't be so hard on yourself, sister. You also have had dragons to slay. But I will add that the offspring you and Kentwood produce will be completely adorable," Millington said with a chuckle.

"**B**ennett, there you are! Just the person I was seeking," said Lady Sophia as she entered the game room of Audrey Manor.

The game room was very open and airy. The ceiling to floor windows hosted a view overlooking the vast ornamental gardens and mazes. The rich oak floors creaked when you walked on them, and the walls were adorned with trophy wild game. A massive, ancient fireplace with an impressive, mounted Monarch stag head above it was surrounded by a leather furniture set – two armchairs, a long settee framed with an oriental rug – a center point for having conversations. One corner of the room hosted a chess table, and in the center was an exquisite billiards table engraved with oceanside carvings depicting the cliffs with sailing vessels out in the Channel.

Kentwood was standing beside the billiards table. He picked up his stick and said, "Cousin, what brings you here? Willing to wager a game and lose?"

Dunning a smile and swishing her way to stand on the opposite side of the table from Kentwood, Sophia responded, "No, you never taught me how to play. Perhaps Lord Miles will." She wanted to ruffle Kentwood's feathers.

At the mention of Lord Miles, Kentwood growled. "You need to proceed with caution, my dearest cousin. Lord Miles is a rake, and he knows how to use his charms to get what he wants. I would hate to see your heart bleeding," Kentwood said in a rather fatherly voice.

Rebutting his comments Sophia lifted her chin, "Oh cousin, do not fret over my disposition. It is you I am most concerned about. When are you going to tell Miss Lane that you love her?"

Kentwood's cue stick went flying above his target, missing his shot completely. He forgot how his cousin didn't care what came out of her sauce box. "My personal matters are not up for debate." Kentwood was frazzled.

Sophia decided it was the perfect time to keep prodding. "You have been sulking the halls and grounds of this fine manor since my arrival. I see the way you look at her. I see how she steals glances of you. I may be young, but I can see when two people are in love. So, tell me cousin, do you love her?"

Slightly rocking back and forth on his heels, Kentwood placed his cue stick to perch straight up from the floor and rested his hands and chin upon it. "What do you apprehend about love?"

Sophia positioned both hands on the pool table and stared Kentwood down. "Love can leave you breathless. It leaves you wanting for more. It ravishes your senses. Love makes you ache with the need to share your life with that person. You can never imagine living without him. Love makes you stronger, weaker, braver, and foolish all at once. It's all consuming."

"Sophia, stay away from Lord Miles," said Kentwood with a steely voice. "He will do nothing but break your heart and ruin you for whomever the man is that follows his wake."

Sophia shook her head and regained her composure. With her nose tilted higher and lips pursed together she said, "Well, we are not talking about me. The question presented was whether or not you love Miss Lane."

The definition of love that his cousin recited to him was everything he felt for Miss Lane and more. *Damnation!* Setting his cue stick on the table he asked, "What am I to do? She is below my rank and station in every way. A marriage to her will cause a scandal and she refused to be my mistress."

With hands on her hips, Sophia scolded him. "Bennett David Wheeler! Did you seriously offer her to be your paramour? What were you thinking? Miss Lane is more than that and you know it!"

Raking his hand through his thick umber brown hair, Kentwood frustratedly declared, "I didn't offer anything. She assumed that I intended for her to be my concubine and squashed it before I even had a cue of the notion."

"The answer is simple. Marry her. Make her your Duchess. Your bile headed father is no longer here to stop you. You hold all the cards in your hands. There is nothing stopping you but your own folly of having a reputation to uphold. Dukes can do what they want. Do not miss this chance at love and happiness. I beg you," pleaded Sophia. She was doing her darndest to convince Kentwood to follow his heart, secretly hoping it would help her in the near future with Kentwood's acceptance of Miles.

Looking perplexed, Kentwood said, "I do believe it is time to join the others for dinner." He exited the gaming room, leaving Sophia alone.

Sophia stomped her foot like a spoiled princess and produced a moan of vexation before departing for the dining room.

At the dining table, the first courses were being served. Millington was at the head of the table with Lord Miles to his right and Kentwood to his left. Lady Sophia positioned directly across from Miles, leaving Franny with no choice but to sit opposite of Kentwood. *How will I get through this meal without having to look upon him? Bloody hell. Why did I have to be the last body to enter the room?* Franny wore a very daring, low cut indigo colored gown cinched at the waste with a sash decorated with peacock feathers. Her curving womanhood on full display.

Millington gave his sister a look that said, *"What the fuck are you wearing?"*

"Miss Lane, your gown is stunning. Please share who your modiste is. I promise to keep it a secret," Franny begged.

"I am happy to introduce you to my sarta, Miss Valentina Bellucci. She is a true innovator when it comes to fashion," said Franny.

Miles, who already gulped down his soup, said, "Lady Sophia, have you had your first season?"

With a flirtatious smile, Sophia answered, "I have, Lord Miles. And it saddens me that I was never introduced to you. I daresay a strong, handsome figure like you would be hard to miss by all the meddling mamas."

Miles shrugged his shoulders. "Thank you. It is indeed hard for me. So charming, dashing and all. I try to avoid the mamas," he causally said, acting like the rake he was.

"Perhaps this Miss Bellucci can create next season's gowns and I will have all sorts of men wooing for my attention." Sophia laughed as she took a sip of wine. Resting her goblet on the eggshell white linen tablecloth, she asked, "Miss Lane, the Italian language in my opinion is the most romantic sounding of all. How does one say *I love you* in your native tongue?"

Franny's mouth opened but it wasn't her voice that came out. It was Miles. Directly his gaze at Lady Sophia he said in a sultry voice, "Ti voglio bene, Tesoro."

Sophia slowly placed her hand on her heart. "Oh my, that truly is romantic."

Kentwood glared across the table at Miles and loudly cleared his throat.

"What? I happen to be fluent in Italian. Also, in French, German, and most importantly, the language of love," said Miles, nonchalantly, as he stared at Lady Sophia. He was irredeemable.

"Lord Miles, that is most accomplished and impressive. Is it not, Bennett?" Sophia raised a brow toward her cousin in hopes of gaining some minuscule of approval for Miles as a suitor.

"Bennett?"

Good Lord, my cousin and Lord Miles probably have already compromised themselves. Hopefully not to the point that I have with Miss Lane. Kentwood huffed a sigh and annoyingly answered Sophia as he raised his wine to his lips. "Most indeed."

The next plate arrived. Salmon with capers and potatoes. "Millington, your cook is excellent. Please tell the kitchen staff of my high regards," applauded Kentwood.

"I will. Thank you, Kentwood," Millington said as he stabbed a savory, herbed potato with his fork. "The herbs we grow in the orangery came from Italy. We are very fortunate to have such delicacies at our whim."

"It is unfortunate that the *ton* doesn't provide adequate dinners such as this at the many soirees we must endure during the season," said Kentwood as he enjoyed the fish. "Do you host a ball? It would be a shame to miss it if the food is as excellent as it is this evening."

Franny wiped the corners of her mouth. "We have not."

Raising a quizzical brow, Kentwood eyed Franny and asked, "I do not recall you in town for a season, Miss Lane. When were you presented?"

Franny thought, *"Why is Kentwood bringing this topic into the conversation? He knows why I detest London society."*

Miles and Edward looked at Franny. She never had a season, nor was she ever presented to the Queen. After father died, Franny was too busy raising her brothers and running the estates. At her age, what was the point? Noticing the change in Franny's manner, Miles redirected the conversation, "When you ponder on the subject of the *ton*, the only people at this table that really belong to the *ton* is my family."

"Pardon?" Kentwood was irritated and reacted with slighted voice, "I daresay the Kentwood family has been part of the *ton* since before yours, Lord Miles. We go back to William the Conqueror."

"Forgive me, Kentwood. No doubt, you are part of the upper crest of society. It's the spelling of the names. For example, we are Milling*TON*'s. You are Kent*WOOD*'s. Therefore, not really a member of the *TON*. There should be events for each specific family ending."

Everyone appeared confused.

Miles explained more in detail, "There are the *ton* families like Millington, Aubrington, Lansington and Borrington that would attend *ton* events."

Lady Sophia interrupted with her own logic. With a one finger up in the air, she set down her wine and said, "I have concluded the Borrington's are the least boring family within the *ton* just to spite their very name."

With lustful eyes, Miles responded straight to Sophia, "That is a wise observation, Lady Sophia."

Kentwood growled with disgust. "Oh, for heaven's sake, please get on with this nonsensical lesson."

Miles continued, "You have *wood* families, such as Kentwood and Linwood that would attend *wood* events. Then there are the *burn* and *born* families, like Dearborn and Bayburn. The *dale* and *land* families, such as Westland and Hillsdale."

"And you can't forget the *son* families, like Harrison and Williamson," Millington said with a chuckle. He chimed in with his contribution to the ridiculous conversation just to perturb Kentwood.

"Yes, thank you, my favorite brother," said Miles.

"I am your only brother." Millington was aggravated by the behavior of Miles. *He's lucky he is my brother, or he would be out on his rear right now.*

Kentwood did not appreciate being bested and decided to throw all this idiotic logic out the window by asking, "So would you consider George Washing*TON* a part of THE *ton*?"

The room went silent. Everyone looked at each other and all started to marginally shake their heads, *no.* Laughter filled the room.

Franny sat a little straighter in her chair and blurted out, "However, when you really consider all the close kin in one season, it's best not to separate seasons by last name endings. It could lead to a lot of first and second cousin unions, and we all have witnessed how those offspring turn out to be."

"Mad," said everyone.

More laughter fell upon the dinner party. The wine was working its magic.

With his wine stem in the air Kentwood said, "This truly is the most absurd dinner conversation."

Everyone responded, "Here, here!"

A footman entered the room with the evening's dessert. A lemon and black olive cake with a chocolate dipping sauce on the side. Franny lightly clapped her hands together with excitement. "Yes, this is our latest creation for the upcoming cooking and baking instruction book that centers on the use of Mama Maria products."

Kentwood showed a face of disgust and with one eyebrow raised he inquired, "You use your servants to create the materials for the cookbook and then reap the reward?"

Millington sat back in his seat while the footman placed the dessert in front of him and proudly corrected Kentwood, "The staff reaps the majority of profits from our cookbooks and even gardening books."

"Yes, most of the revenues made from anything the staff here at Audrey Manor contribute toward Mama Maria products go into a kitty. The funds are used to help the village with items such as assistance with financial distress, making repairs to buildings, and so forth," declared Miles as he ate a piece of cake.

"We recently used some of the funds to send Cook's son, Mr. Bryant, to university. He is most excellent with numbers," said Franny.

Millington took a bite of the cake, rested his fork down and said, "It is our hope he comes back to Audrey Manor and works as a man-of-affairs."

Kentwood asked, "Who invented this brilliant idea of a community pot of monies and the training of potential staff?"

Miles gave Franny a most enduring brotherly smile and replied, "Franny. She is most innovated and thoughtful."

Kentwood stared at Miss Lane with desperation and admiration at the same time. "Forgive me for jumping to conclusions this evening. Once again, I am in complete awe of you, Miss Lane. Most indeed."

Franny blushed. "Thank you, Your Grace. There is nothing to forgive. We are all guilty of surmising events, especially me," Franny said with a slight smile and a voice that asked forgiveness from him. Catching the quiet truce that Franny offered him, Kentwood slightly raised his glass to her and nodded his head with a grin that highlighted his adorable dimples.

Chapter Ten

In his chamber, Kentwood poured himself a nightcap of his family's Scottish whisky. Illegal as it was, he managed to hide a still or two around his estate in Scotland. His mother's family played a key role in making whisky a popular, naughty drink in and around the *ton*. Kentwood pursued making the drink a legal substance by hopefully passing policy through Parliament. He was optimistic he could make his stills into a business venture. He even had drawn various label designs portraying the brand, McNevin Scotch – a dedication to his mother's family.

Throwing his coat over the chair, he discarded his boots, socks, and shirt. He washed his face and hands. Wearing only his drawers, Kentwood walked to the fire and stoked it. He started wondering, *"What was the hidden message in the ending exchange with Miss Lane at tonight's dinner? Do I dare hope there is a prospect of making Miss Lane my Duchess? Does she think about me as I think of her?"*

Kentwood cleared his thoughts as he drank the last drop of whisky. If his stay at Audrey Manor had taught him one thing that would be to not hypothesis scenarios that may never come to fruition.

Franny wasn't sure what she was doing. Every night, since the night she and Kentwood gained all carnal knowledge of one another, she would lay in her bed recalling the enchanted moment. She tried to recreate the same exploding sensation that Kentwood made her feel by using her own hand, but it didn't compare. She tried to ignore him, hoping her infatuation would die. It did not. She realized it wasn't just an infatuation after all. It was love. A very powerful, exhilarating love and she wanted to have it with her always.

Standing in front of the door of Kentwood's chamber, she tried in vain to calm her heart. Its tempo was at a faster pace than normal, and her body felt flushed. She whispered, "Don't think. Just act." Without knocking, Franny turned the beehive doorknob and quietly slipped into the room. She slowly put her backside on the door and walked it to a close. Franny gasped. With eyes wide, she took in the sight of Kentwood. He was by the fire, wearing only his short-cut drawers. His hands on the mantle, arms elongated, he slightly leaned his defined muscular body. Corded muscles even outlined the side of his torso. His legs reminded her of the estate's strongest draft horses. The Duke of Kentwood was an enigma.

Kentwood glanced at Franny and in a low, seductive, hushed tone he said, "Miss Lane, what are you doing here?"

"I must be dreaming," he thought. Miss Lane leaning back against the entry door with her hands behind her back. Her long hair of loose curls framed her face. She was wearing a nightgown of red silk that clung to her like a winter's glove. A matching-colored dressing gown was over it, tied just below the neckline with a simple black bow. She looked ethereal. Little Buddy immediately stood at attention. This time, nothing Kentwood could do would stand him down.

Franny curtsied. "Your Grace." She carefully walked closer to him. They never took their eyes off each other.

Kentwood made one stride to meet her. "You have been avoiding me."

Feeling a bit foolish, Franny looked down. "Yes. I have."

Kentwood reached for her, cupping his hand on the side of her cheek. Tired of playing games, Kentwood asked, "What is it you want, Miss Lane?"

Bringing her head up, Franny placed her fingers on his bicep and responded in a whisper, "You." She turned her head and kissed the inside of his palm. "I want you, Bennett."

Raising both her wrists, Kentwood kissed the whisps of her scars and declared with an anxious voice, "Miss Lane, I love you."

Admiring his eyes, she opened her heart and soul to him and confidently said, "I love you too."

Kentwood leaned his forehead down to hers. With a smile he asked for more assurance, "You... you do?"

"Oh Bennett, I'm so sorry. I have been so dimwitted. The emotions you stirred simply terrified me. There are no words to explain it. I want to be with you always." Franny rubbed her cheek against his.

Kentwood grabbed her hands. "My darling, let us take care of another in this life. I never want to be apart from you. What we have is something rare. I daresay not many married couples have this kind of love. Marry me, Miss Lane. Be my Duchess."

Franny placed her hands on his bare, brut chest and caressed down to the buttons of his drawers. She bit her bottom lip and gave Kentwood a wicked grin. She opened the front of his fold and released Little Buddy. Going down on her knees she touched his shaft. She took one finger and ran it downward from the top to the base. Then she kissed the tip of it.

Bennett breathed out, combined with a bit of a moan, and spoke, "Franny, I asked you to marry me, not be my mistress." He gently lifted her face up.

Looking up at him with a mischievous grin, she said, "Why can't I be both your wife and your mistress? And you shall call me, Miss Lane."

Franny licked the tip of Little Buddy again. She gripped his shaft and lightly stroked it. *Fascinating.* With her grip at the base, Franny placed Little Buddy into her mouth and proceeded to suck in as much of him as she could. Bennett caressed the hair on top of her head, guiding her on what to do, his breathing increased. "Dear God, woman. You are a marvelous wonder."

The bedchamber door swooshed open. Franny was on her knees performing the wicked act with her back to the door while Kentwood was in full view of the newly arrived intruder.

Millington.

"Kentwood, join me for a... what the bloody hell?!" Millington was shocked, to say the least.

Does this family not knock when entering a private chamber? Kentwood recalled how Franny didn't knock just a few moments previous. Swiftly bringing Franny up to a standing position, Kentwood buttoned up his drawers using Franny as a shield and turned Franny around to face her brother.

Kentwood exclaimed, "Christ Millington, do you know how to knock?!

Still in the doorway, Millington was bent over holding his midsection. "Oh God. Oh. My. God. I am going to be sick." He started dry heaving. Not daring to look at Franny and Kentwood, Millington continued, "Oh, my God, I can't unsee that! What the bloody hell!"

Franny closed her eyes and took a deep breath before confronting her younger brother. *Inhale.* She smelled Kentwood's scent of sandalwood and soap. The aroma calmed her. Franny pictured herself embraced in Bennett's arms and standing near the oceanside cliffs looking across the Channel. *Exhale.* With her head held high and nose tilted slightly up, Franny decided to scold her brother like the big sister she was, "Edward please calm yourself. You are causing a scene."

Millington was dumbfounded. Raking his hands through his hair he exulted, "I'm causing a scene? So, I take it you have agreed to be his mistress. Franny, this is beneath you." Millington pointed to Kentwood and angrily directed, "I will see you at dawn with blades."

"Dearest, there will be no dueling in the morn. We must calm ourselves before the whole of the household staff assumes a fire and come running to aid us." Franny stepped toward Millington trying her best to defuse the potential explosion and keep a scandal from happening.

In the bedchamber down the hall, Lord Miles sweetly kissed the crown of the naked, blonde goddess all wrapped up in his arms. Miles and Lady Sophia were under the bedcovers, arms and legs tangled, their bodies producing the only heat they needed to keep warm. The chamber's fire had gone cold over an hour ago. "Oh, my beautiful Sophia, I am under your spell. As soon as I saw you step out of the carriage upon your arrival, I fell in love with you." Miles was besotted.

Grabbing the hand of Miles, Sophia intertwined her fingers with his and said, "I had no notion one could feel this way. It's completely magical. I do not want to leave this bed. However, I must make haste and return to my chamber before we are discovered."

Sophia planted her feet on the ground from the bed to retrieve her nightgown.

A lot of commotion was coming from the hall. "Well, my darling, it appears there is a fuss happening down the hall. Let's leave together and act like we both came running from our quarters to see what the excitement is all about," said Miles. He jumped around putting his trousers on and threw a shirt over his head.

Puzzled, Sophia asked, "You don't think there is a fire?"

Helping Sophia secure her housecoat, Miles answered, "No, not a fire. At least not the kind that burns a house down." He continued with a wink, "I think we are not the only ones to be playing bed-sport games tonight."

Miles and Sophia quickly walked around the corner of the wing and came to a stop before Kentwood's bedchamber. They stood behind Millington who was in the doorway. "What is the meaning of all this?" Miles asked with a slight smile. He had his arm wrapped around Lady Sophia in a tender, protective embrace.

Millington turned. It was clear to him that Miles was up to no good. He looked at Miles and Sophia and noticed they both appeared thoroughly ravished. Millington's eyes squinted, his lips pursed together as he stared down his younger, rouge of a brother. In a grim, lowered voice he grumbled out the side of his mouth, "What the devil? You two as well? Please remove yourself from her person, now Miles."

Miles ignored his brother and kept his arm around Sophia's backside. Millington was sure he was losing his mind. The blood in his body rushed to his brain. Even his ears started to burn. Glancing back and forth between the couples. "Am I the only person with any sense of decorum in this house?"

In an effort to rectify the situation and avoid any strife from her cousin, Sophia exclaimed, "My Lord, that is completely rude and uncalled for. Why I met Lord Miles in my pursuit to investigate the commotion. One never knows, it might have been a fire. Thank the stars it was not."

More footsteps approached the group. Griz and Cecilia came around the corner together in a hurried fashion. Millington immediately noticed they both seemed quite disheveled and guilty of something – the nervous way the two looked at each other. He thought, *"Surely, not them as well."*

Griz and Cecilia came upon the scene and stopped before the spur-of-the-moment party. Cecilia gave a customary curtsy. Griz bowed and asked, "My lords. My ladies. Is there a fire? An intruder? How may we be of service?"

Kentwood stepped into the hall to address everyone. He was responsible for this fiasco and decided to take charge of the situation.

"CEASE!"

All eyes turned to Kentwood. He addressed Franny's brothers, "Millington, Lord Miles, I have asked Miss Lane to marry me, and she said yes... I think." He glanced over to Franny who was still in the bedchamber.

Franny went to Kentwood's side and answered, "I did not answer your question, Your Grace," Biting her bottom lip and trying not to grin, she continued, "My mouth was full just a moment ago." Her cheeks immediately flushed red. Kentwood stared at her in disbelief and started to laugh. Millington put his hand across his mouth to keep his accounts from spewing out.

Miles was loving the interlude. To see his brother so distraught over whatever it was he saw, well, the mind can only wonder. Miles added to the exchange, "Yes, nighttime morsels are simply the best. Just a nimble here and a nimble there."

"Do shut up, Miles," Millington scolded his brother with a growl.

Putting an arm around the back of Franny, Kentwood brushed the hair from the side of her cheek and asked, "Darling, please say you'll be my Duchess."

"Yes, I will marry you, my sweet Bennett," Franny sweetly answered.

Lady Sophia blurted out, "Capital!" With arms wide open she embraced Franny. "We shall be sisters soon. Well... cousins, but more like sisters. I'm so happy for you both." Sophia almost gave away the idea that she wanted to marry Lord Miles to the present company. It did not go unnoticed. Miles stared at Sophia with a bit of shock and bewilderment. *"Hum, perhaps he isn't in love with me after all,"* Sophia told herself. She worried she had made an enormous error of judgement this past week during her stay at Audrey Manor. The look on her lover's disturbed face was alarming. Sophia was debating whether or not Miles loved her, even though he repeatedly confessed he did. *He probably just said those sweet words to get me under him. I am a fool.*

Millington's words interrupted Sophia's negative thoughts. "Kentwood, you and I will go in the morning to secure a special license. We must keep this from becoming an unwanted news story," Millington decreed. "Now everyone back to their chambers. To your own individual chambers. Audrey Manor is not a brothel!"

Millington observed everyone depart and suddenly he felt very alone.

Chapter Eleven

Everyone stood on the gravel drive of the main entrance. The grounds shimmered with morning dew and the air had a hint of rosemary and sea salt. Blake, along with a stable boy, brought two stallions for Millington and Kentwood. As soon as they saddled up, they were off to obtain a special license for Kentwood and Franny to wed.

"Oh Franny, this is spine-tingling excitement. *Eke!*" Lady Sophia couldn't hide how excited she was to see her cousin marry Franny. Grabbing Franny's arm she continued, "As soon the gents depart, we must have tea and make a list. I shall be your Maid of Honour and will see to every detail. You need not worry about thing."

A bit of laughter floated through the air. With a big smile of joy, Franny patted Sophia's hand and said, "Lady Sophia, you may plan away. I am more than happy to relinquish those duties to you."

Sophia jumped a little in her step, trying to hold down her excitement.

"Rider approaching my lord," Griz announced. He was helping the groomsman hold onto Millington's spirited horse, Maximus.

"I daresay Millington, you are either one hell of a rider or a very foolish one to call that horseflesh your trusted steed," said Kentwood as he recalled his neck-breaking ride with the horse in the rain. A fond memory for Kentwood, for it was the day he first kissed Franny. He lovingly peered over at his impending bride. She was wearing his favorite color on her - crimson red. He couldn't wait to get her naked and under him or perhaps her on top of him. And there goes Little Buddy.

Damnation.

Franny glanced at Kentwood and noticed he was starting to get a bit bulkier in the front of his pants. She covered her nose and mouth, pretending to sneeze in order to stop herself from laughing out loud. Franny mouthed the words, *"I love you,"* to Kentwood.

In the distance a rider was approaching with great haste. Miles came aside Millington, glanced at his brother and said. "What do you think this is about, dear brother?"

Millington's face was washed over with extreme concern. He responded to Miles, "Whatever it is, it's not good."

Dressed in military regalia, the rider came to a hard stop that resulted in gravel spraying upward in a frenzy. He quickly dismounted his horse and yelled, "Lord Miles Lane?"

"That is I." Miles stepped forward.

With a bow, the rider presented Miles with a sealed note.

The rider continued, "The Duke of Millington?"

Millington stepped forward and responded, "Here!" The rider gave Millington the missive and immediately mounted his horse and sped off.

Everyone was huddled in a circular formation. Saying the question everyone wanted the answer for, Lady Sophia boldly asked, "What is it?"

Miles recognized the note's seal straight away. "It's from the Home Office." He broke the seal and opened the note. Upon reading, his face turned to ash and his arms dropped to his sides. He was looking at Sophia, but his stare was blank – his eyes gave no emotion. "I have been called to take my place with the Guards on the Continent." His voice trailed off when he read the last line, "In a fortnight."

Oomph.

Sophia's body slammed into Miles as she ran into his arms, embracing him into a lover's death grip. He gently pushed her slightly back and took both his hands to her face. Tears welling up in her eyes, she stared at him. With a tender smile he addressed her with a benevolent voice, "Oh, my sweet, please don't cry. Marry me. Please do me the greatest honor and be my wife."

Miles stood in shock by the sudden news that he was going to battle. Selfishly, all he could think of was how he needed Sophia to be his wife. At that moment, he only saw Sophia. The others were nonexistent. Still delicately holding Sophia's face with both hands, he gently pulled his lips down to hers and kissed her as if it were the last kiss they would ever share together.

CRACK!

"What the fuuuu... freaking frat was that for?!" Miles let out a bitter shout, rubbing his face where the assailant's fist impounded his flesh. It was Kentwood.

"How does that feel Lord Miles? Not very well, does it." Kentwood recalled it wasn't long ago that the knuckles of Miles left imprinted marks on his face and well deserved, he must admit, for ruining Miss Lane. An eye for an eye, Kentwood thought.

Miles announced, "I love her!"

Kentwood was getting ready to unleash another blow. Franny was not going to have her betrothed and brother come to fisticuffs right in front of her. She stepped between Kentwood and Miles. Trying to diffuse the situation, Franny looked at the two lovers and said, "You both are very young, and this is merely an infatuation that will pass. Let's not be hasty."

Staring straight at Sophia and knowing what he was about to say would cause another punch from Kentwood, Miles braced himself and declared, "I ruined her."

CRACK!

Kentwood knocked Miles down to the ground. Millington joined Franny and also stepped-in between Miles and Kentwood. He had his large stump of an arm holding Kentwood back.

Recalling the words Miles previously used against him, Kentwood asked Miles in a low, very snippy voice, "Did you pump and dump? Every lord of the peerage knows to pump and dump." Then he took the palm of his hand and swatted Miles across the back of the head like a grandmother who just caught her grandson stealing another biscuit.

"Kentwood, darling, that is enough. Please," begged Franny. Shaking her arms out in front of her, Franny continued in a nervous voice, "I mean... surely one time is not going to produce an unwanted outcome. Right?" Thinking back to her interlude with Kentwood, she was also hoping the one-time mishap of his army of seed didn't implant themselves. *What if they did? A baby with the man I am about to marry. A family to love and cherish. I love him so much.* Franny's heart was smiling.

Franny directed her words to Sophia, "Mayhap your version of one's ruination is not really that terrible."

Then looking at Miles with the face of a disgruntled governess she continued, "Particularly, in the eyes of an innocent. The notion of being ruined is hardly noted by just a few kisses stolen."

Franny turned to Sophia and asked, "Lady Sophia, you have graced us with your person for just a sennight. I mean, how ruined can you be?" Franny nervously chuckled.

Sophia gave Miles a sinful grin and said, "Oh… I've been ruined more than once. In fact, I am rather very, thoroughly ruined."

Bringing an elbow up under his body to prompt himself up, Miles whispered, "I love you."

Millington gave his brother a hand to help him off the ground. Miles quickly came to Sophia's side. "Darling, I love you. I never want to be apart from you, but now circumstances are saying otherwise. If I am going off to war, I need to marry you now. You could be carrying my child. Our child. If something happens to me, I want to be sure that you and the child have the protection of my name. I couldn't bear being on foreign soil knowing that I didn't protect your reputation. To marry you would make me the happiest of men. Please marry me."

Kentwood looked back and forth between Miles and Sophia and grunted, "As much as I *detest* this annoying man and his lack of propriety, he makes a valid point. Sophia, if marriage to Lord Miles is what you truly want, I will support you. But if you are at all uncertain and only marrying him because of the possibility of a child and not for affection, I will support you and the child if that is the case."

"Yes," Sophia said. Her face beamed with joy as she answered Miles.

"Yes?" Miles was breathless with emotion. His heart felt like it was going to pop out right from his chest. He placed his palm over his heart as if he were trying to keep it in place.

"Yes. I will marry you. I love you too, Miles," declared Sophia.

"Capital!" Miles embraced Sophia and spun her around, bringing her down into a sweet kiss.

Franny entwined her arm around Kentwood's impressive bicep. She rested her head on the side of his shoulder. Kentwood lovingly caressed her hand. He spoke to Millington, "It seems we are in need of two special licenses. We can work out all the marriage contracts upon our return. What say you, Millington?"

"Millington?"

Pale faced and standing before everyone in complete shock, Millington looked like he had just discovered his favorite pup had gone on to a greater reward. He couldn't help but heed an overwhelming sensation of guilt for everything that had occurred. From the ruination of his sister and Lady Sophia to not being able to prevent his dearest brother from going to war, he failed them. Millington's missive gave information of how Napoleon escaped his imprisoned exile. The arse of a man had gathered up forces again on the Continent. Millington was everything he feared to become in life – a total failure. Trying to hide his true façade, Millington said with a forced smirk, "Yes, two licenses.

My apologies. After witnessing all this besottedness, I am praying I'm not next."

"If you could be so lucky, brother," Miles said as he embraced Sophia once again.

"Blake, please ready a horse for Lord Miles immediately," said Millington as he mounted Maximus.

As the menfolk took off down the gravel drive, Franny walked back to the house, arm-in-arm with Sophia. She consoled Sophia in an enduring, sisterly matter, "Dearest, it is I that will be your Maid of Honour. You and Miles shall marry first so you can have as much time together before he takes leave. Now, what are your favorite flowers? We have a wedding to plan!"

Chapter Twelve

One Week Later

Inside the quaint stone village church, the rafters were laced with tule that held pale pink roses and sow bread twisted into a garland. White bows with evergreens lined the tops of the pews. The reverend declared, "I now pronounce husband and wife. You may kiss the bride." Miles secured his arm around Sophia's back and brought his lips down to hoover just above hers. With a wicked smile he suddenly dipped a squealing Sophia and kissed her. The packed sanctuary went into an uproar of cheers and salutations for the newly minted Mr. and Mrs. Lane.

The bride wore a pastel blue, capped-sleeved silk evening gown, embroidered with white chenille thread and silk ribbon that portrayed tiny doves. Sophia finished the ensemble with white-laced eyelet gloves and the Wheeler tiara, which boasted a round opal at the center point, adorned with diamond scrolls throughout. Her blonde locks were styled in a loosely curled Grecian knot with a few wisps framing her face. The groom was very handsome in his officer reds accessorized with a calvary sword.

The wedding breakfast was a spectacular pageantry of food, champagne, flowers, and greens. The guests enjoyed a three-course meal featuring Dover Sole, a flaky small fish with a sweet, mild flavor. During the wedding planning, Miles and Sophia discovered they both loved riding to the cliffs that overlooked the English Channel. The fish served at the reception was a symbol of their shared love of the sea. The sound and smells of the ocean soothed their souls. Miles told Sophia whenever she desperately missed him, she should go to the cliffs and send him a message into the waves and wind. He promised that he would do the same from the other side of the Channel.

As the head of the family, Millington was seated at the end of the elongated dining table. He sat back and drank his wine, pondering over all the love seated before him. There was his brother and his new bride at the center, along with his sister and her betrothed who were to be wed in three days' time. Even Cecilia and Griz enjoyed the day with the family and sat at the table, looking very besotted. Millington highly suspected that the two were canoodling. The other guests included the Earl of Warwick's widow, Lady Tabitha, and three of his sons, Thomas (son number two), Robert (son number three) and William (son number four), who was the Best Man. At the end of the week the three sons of

Lady Tabitha will be setting off for war along with Miles. Another pain of guilt shot through Millington.

"I daresay, Edward, you are looking rather glum for such a happy occasion. Perhaps you were hoping to settle on Lady Sophia's heart?" Countess Warwick, who was seated to Millington's right, teased him.

"No. Miles won that heart as soon as she stepped out of the carriage," Millington said as he drank the wedding wine.

"Perhaps one day Edward, you will be just as besotted as Lord Miles, and from my observations, the Duke of Kentwood as well," said the Countess as she tilted her head in a meddling manner.

"Lady Tabitha, Countess, I will never be besotted. In fact, I am beginning to despise the word with every ounce of my being." With that confession, Millington swallowed down the rest of his wine.

Bayberry Hall, Kent – Four Days Later

"Good morning, my Duchess."

"Good morning, husband."

Franny was encased in Bennett's body. He sweetly kissed the top of her head, taking in the sight of his beautiful wife as the morning sunlight beamed on her causing streaks of reddish highlights to shine in her hair. He never felt so at ease and happy in his life. Bennett's stomach growled.

"My dear husband, you sound like you are famished. Must be from last night's rigorous activities. By the way, you performed your duties very well," Franny said as she smoothed her palm over Bennett's defined chest.

Bennett responded with a jest as he hugged Franny closer to his chest, "Yes, indeed. I am a master of the marital bed." He then sat up and continued, "I do believe some rations are outside the door. I shall go see."

Without acquiring a robe, Bennett proudly strutted from the bed stark naked. Franny put her hand to her mouth to muffle her laughter. She was so in love with him. He came back into bed with a tray containing tea, bread, hard boiled eggs, fruits, and marmalade. Franny sat up to enjoy the morsels as her husband fed her. When he placed a strawberry into her mouth, she grabbed his hand, took two of his fingers and sucked off the fruit's juices.

Little Buddy responded kindly and was hard as a rock. Franny smiled and said, "Your Grace, please control your other brain. I am afraid he only ever wants one thing."

Bennett looked down at Little Buddy and said, "His name is Little Buddy and when it comes to the sight of you being wicked, I have no control over him."

"We must rename him. As I said before, he is hardly little. I do believe he deserves a reward for last night's gallantry." Without hesitation, Franny pushed Bennett onto his back and proceeded to kiss his chest, working her way down his body. She then took some marmalade and dropped a small dab on the tip of Little Buddy.

"Oh, dear God, woman. How did I get so lucky?" Bennett lost his breath. The sight of Franny practicing such naughty deeds surprised him – in a good way. Franny then took him in her mouth and proceed to suck his cock until he pulled her head from him just before he was going to come.

Franny protested, "I wasn't done."

"No, we are not done," responded Bennett as he sat up and placed a searing kiss of passion on her lips. He then guided her to straddle him. He directed Little Buddy into her canal and plunged. They both gasped at the sensation. Both of them were seated up and facing each other. Franny wrapped her legs around Bennett's waist almost as if she were sitting with her legs crossed. Bennett took her hips into his hands and guided her slowing up and down on his shaft. He found her pearl and teased it as Franny rocked back and forth. He held her close and took one of her nipples into his mouth, lightly flicking the tip with his tongue. Franny trembled with pleasure, coating his cock with her wetness.

She framed his face with both her hands and kissed him. Placing both palms on his chest, she leaned forward on him and physically pushed him down on his back. Franny grabbed both his hands and held them down at the sides of this face, pinning him to the bed. She then rode him with fury, wanting to give him the same pleasure that he so unselfishly, constantly gave her. The position made her feel powerful. Franny watched Bennett as his body released his seed within her. His eyes told her how much he loved her. She slowed her tempo to a stop and rested her head on his chest, taking in the beating of his heart.

Bennett wrapped his arms around her and said, "I never thought I would know what love was. You bring so much happiness into my life. I love you." He sweetly kissed the crown of her head. "That reminds me, I have something for you." Bennett reached under the bed and placed a small, oak box beside Franny. "Open it, please." Franny opened the box and pulled out a pearl choker and an additional longer string of pearls. The beauty of them took her breath away. "They were my mothers. She would've liked you very much," Bennett said as he delicately placed the pearls around Franny's neck.

"Oh, Bennett. They are exquisite," Franny said as she touched the pearls to her naked chest.

"They are Scottish pearls, handed down from my ancestors. They look incredible on you, my Duchess." Bennett kissed Franny's forehead.

Scooting closer to Bennett on bed and giving a playful smile, Franny said, "I have something for you as well, my husband."

"Are you telling me that last night and this morning wasn't your present?" Bennett joked as he brought his arms around his wife.

Giving Bennett a sweet smile, Franny continued, "My gift for you isn't quite here yet."

"You are a gift to me every day, Francesca Wheeler, Duchess of Kentwood," declared Bennett as he kissed her softly on the lips and reached for some more food. Popping a fresh strawberry into his mouth he asked, "So... when will this gift be here?"

Tilting her head to the side, she spoke lackadaisically, "Oh... in about eight months."

Bennett stopped the next tidbit of food he was about to eat in midair. The color rushed from his face. He could feel the blood in his body pushing downward and out of his being.

A babe.

"A baby? So soon? Are you sure? We've hardly begun trying." Bennett was a bit shocked.

Tears started to well in Franny's eyes. She nervously spoke as she bit down on a fingernail, "It is very soon, but I am most certain. Apparently, Little Buddy is most potent. Are you unhappy?"

Grabbing Franny's face with both his hands, Bennett set out to make amends for his foolish reaction. "Oh, my dearest. I am beyond thrilled. I am so sorry for that response. Just wasn't expecting the news so soon. Forgive your simpleton of a husband. You have made me the happiest of men." He again sweetly kissed her lips. "I love you."

"I love you too, Bennett."

Epilogue

Bayberry Hall, Kent – Five Years Later

Gently rubbing her ever growing midsection and placing a hand behind her back for more support, Franny watched from the sideline as Bennett and Blake, the stable master they shared with Millington, gave riding lessons to the twins. The oldest twin was a girl named Lady Evelyn Maria Wheeler and the boy was the Marquess of Pentwater, Lord John Miles Wheeler, the future Duke of Kentwood. When Franny gave birth, she wasn't surprised there were two babies. She constantly commented that it felt like a fencing match was happening inside her as she increased. At five years old, the twins were very tall for their age. Most people mistook them for being eight, even nine years of age. Not surprising, since she and Bennett were blessed with such tall stature.

"Mama, soon I will be racing thoroughbreds and jumping hedges," declared Lady Evelyn, who was the daredevil of the two siblings. Strong-minded and stubborn, a beauty with wavy, chestnut brown hair and delightful eyes of chocolate, she won over anyone's heart when she flashed her sweet smile that highlighted one sole dimple on her right cheek.

"Dearest, you must be patient and wait until you are bit older. I shalt not argue that someday you shall race horses and jump hedges with the greatest of finesse," Franny acclaimed.

Lord John reminded Franny of her younger brother, Edward. He had her dark hair and hazel eyes, but his personality was already stoic like a duke with a bit of mischief mixed in. He loved to correct Evelyn and said, "Sister, you are a lady. You are not allowed to race horses. Papa, she should be learning to ride sidesaddle."

Bennett looked at Franny and their nonverbal facial exchange said, *"here we go again."* The twins loved to spar with each other, much to the dismay of their parents, but Franny wouldn't change a thing. She loved everything about her family. Her adult life was vastly different from her depressing childhood. Franny said a prayer of thanks to God every evening for all the blessings He bestowed on her.

"Oh." Franny lost her breath with the latest contraction. The pains grew increasingly closer together. She let out a silent exhale and took a cleansing breath. "Bennett, I am going to go back inside and…oh dear!" As she started to waddle off, her waters ruptured. She stopped.

Bennett raced over to assist her. "That will be all for the lessons today my children. Come, let's help mother to the house," he said as he directed the children to come by his side.

"I will see to the horses and send a missive immediately to Cecilia," yelled Blake. He understood perfectly well what had just occurred. Afterall, he was a father with eight children. Cecilia was the village midwife and still the dearest friend to Franny. Griz and Cecilia married. Millington gifted a cottage to them that sat between Audrey Manor and Bayberry Hall, allowing Griz and Cecilia to work at either estate and be present at all the family events.

"Are you sure you can walk to the house?" Bennett placed a supporting arm around his wife.

"Yes, it is believed that a light walk helps with a faster delivery of the baby," Franny said with reassurance.

As Bennett and Franny walked back to the house, the twins skipped ahead and sang in unison, "Mama had a baby and her head popped off!"

Sarcastically Franny said to Bennett, "Our children are soooo lovely." They burst out in laughter as Franny bent down with another contraction.

"I love you, my Duchess."

"I love you, my Adorable Duke."

Author's Note

Please keep in mind that this book is historical fiction, a genre that elaborates and uses the imagination to portray fictional characters during a particular historical period. *The Adorable Duke* briefly touched on the history of Catholicism in England, the life of Napoleon, the illegal trade and drinking of Scotch during the early 1800s, and the folklore of nursey rhymes.

Catholicism, at one time, was outlawed in England. The Church of England reigned supreme. The Catholic Emancipation occurred with the Catholic Relief Act of 1791, allowing Catholics to worship freely, and set up schools and other institutions, such as convents and abbeys. Lulworth Abbey was an actual abbey established by refuge French monks in 1796.

For a spell, Napoleon Bonaparte was a military leader and emperor of France. The movement to overthrow the French monarchy was inspired by the American's successful fight for freedom from the British in the late 1700s. Napoleon was defeated by allied forces and placed into exile in early 1814. The British government did not want to kill Napoleon for two reasons. First, he surrendered like a gentleman (such a weird notion in today's world), and second, his followers were massive in number and fevered with passion. To kill Napoleon may have led to a rebellion by the working class of England – something the *ton* wanted to avoid at all costs. Napoleon was exiled to Elba. By March 1815, he escaped to France and had realigned his mighty army to wreak havoc on the nobility of Europe. Allied forces once again forced Napoleon to abdicate. He was exiled a second time to the remote island of Saint Helena, in the southern Atlantic Ocean. He died in 1821 from possible stomach cancer.

The alcoholic drink of Scotch was an illegal substance throughout Great Britain until 1823 when the Excise Act was enacted. The British Government finally figured out it could make money by regulating and taxing the industry. Illegal distilleries and smuggling immediately decreased with the new policy.

"Mama had a baby and it's head popped off." Where did this saying come from? More than likely, it came from a nursery rhyme. Some speculate the saying has ties to the French Revolution and the use of the guillotine or perhaps it is related to the Black Death plague that ravished Europe. Next time you read from the classic *Mother Goose Nursey Rhymes* book, check out "Ring Around The Rosie" and "Rock A Bye Baby." Both have dark meanings with "Ring Around

The Rosie" referencing the Black Death and "Rock A Bye Baby" retelling how mothers, who either suffered a stillborn or had an infant die too soon, would place the dead babies in a cradle up in a tree hoping the swaying of the branches would bring the babies back to life. Yikes!

The Adorable Duke ends with Miles and the Brewer Brothers (Thomas, Robert and William) heading across the English Channel to fight Napoleon. What will happen to Miles and Sophia? Will Millington discover a way to bring his brother safely back home? You can find out by reading The Loyal Officer, the second book in the Audrey Manor Series. Go to www.marieleick.com and sign-up to be notified of future book release dates.

Acknowledgements

Thank you for reading *The Adorable Duke*. This experience and the writing process was more fun than I ever imagined. To have the characters and storylines in your imagination illuminate onto a page is thrilling! It feels like I'm sending one of my kids off to school for the first time, just hoping someone will notice them. I couldn't do this without some help. I must start by thanking my wonderful husband. You are my constant confidence booster and champion. Your support and love give me the courage to write. Thank you for believing in me. I love you.

To Amy, Bret, Michelle, Mike, Sally, and Stacey thank you for your listening ears, words of encouragement, and proof-reading eyes. Your friendship means everything, and I am blessed to have you all in my life. Thank you for allowing me to annoy you so much.

Thank you to my children. For your patience while I write and for your words of positivity. I do apologize that you are not allowed to read this book, but some day when you are an adult (like thirty-years-old), you can.

Lastly, please visit your local library. Books can bring about new ideas and help us escape to other worlds. Books can give us hope, wisdom, and courage to conquer anything. Help unlock the magic of reading for others by supporting your local library and literacy efforts in your community.

About the Author

The Adorable Duke is Marie Leick's debut novella. A native of Michigan, she is a graduate of Oakland University where she studied history, focusing on women and children social welfare in England and the United States during the seventeenth and eighteenth centuries.

When not swept away into a different world with a good book, she enjoys the great outdoors with her family during all four seasons that Michigan offers. Her happy place is walking along the shores of a Great Lake collecting Petoskey stones and lake glass.

Connect with Marie Leick and sign-up to be notified of future book release dates at www.marieleick.com.

Coming Soon!

The Loyal Officer

Audrey Manor Series

Book Two

Wheeler House, Mayfair – Late Autumn 1815

She held the tiny, light blue knitted clothing with both hands and pulled it to her face. Breathing in the scent, hoping to smell the innocent, fresh air of an infant, even though the baby never wore it. Perhaps maybe for just a moment, she could hear a cry or maybe see the most beautiful hazel eyes of sea green and blue, but there was never a cry or the sight of his eyes. She felt nothing but a deep pit of nothingness. Completely nothing. An emptiness that constantly lingered beneath her surface. She was dead on the inside. So dead and hollow, she couldn't even shed a tear. Not anymore. Very delicately, as if the yarn would unravel with the slightest of touch, she placed the jumper back in the packing paper and wrapped it up again, leaving her hand to linger on it for a moment before placing it back inside the trunk. She deeply inhaled and wished the world produced better, happier outcomes. Somedays were better than others and sometimes she wouldn't leave her chamber for a week.

Such was life for Lady Sophia Angelica Lane. At just one and twenty years of age, she was sure she had aged to be at least thirty from the past nightmarish several months. Her once curvy body had dissipated with her loss of appetite. In a short period of time, she fell madly in love and married Lord Miles Shelby Lane. He was her knight in shining armor – her wicked gentleman. Sophia wrapped her arms around herself and closed her eyes. Sometimes she could feel him walking up behind her and wrapping his arms around her one last time. She can vaguely recall the touch of his skin on her when they made love. Those memories faded away with every passing day. Sophia brushed her long, sun-kissed blonde hair as she readied for sleep. She blew out the candles in her bedchamber within Wheeler House of Mayfair. With just the low light of the fire, she put her dressing gown over the chair and sulked into the bed. Resting her head on the pillow, she pulled the counterpane over her, hoping she would dream of her sweet Miles kissing her once again.

Knock. Knock.

The hour was late. The reason for knocking on a bedchamber door at this time of night was never for good news. Sophia knew this from experience. The last time she received a knock on her door at night was when a messenger delivered the devasting news that her Miles had perished at Waterloo. The knocking startled her and sent a shiver of fear down her spine. She sat up in her bed, hugging the covers to her chest. "Who is it?"

"It's Keene, milady." Sophia's dainty lady's maid sounded very nervous.

"Enter."

Keene, who stood maybe five feet short, entered the room holding her housecoat with her fists, keeping it wrapped around her body. Her dishwater blonde hair in rags for the night was tucked under her nightcap. "Pardon me milady, there is an officer at the main door. He is seeking an audience with you. He seems to be quite in his cups or something."

"Or something?" Sophia threw back the bedcovers and grabbed her dressing gown. "Is Mr. Felix awake?" Felix was Sophia's trusted Butler.

Assisting Sophia with her slippers, Keene replied, "Yes, Mr. Felix is with the officer as we speak."

Sophia eloquently dashed down the stairs into the foyer. Turning back to Keene asking in a very perturb way, "Well, where is this said officer?"

Felix came into view – the rigid, tall, brut of a butler gave no facial expression. Ever. He would make a perfect King's Guard. Felix bowed to Sophia and declared in his monotoned voice, "The said officer is outside on the steps. Please follow me."

Noting the rain on the windows, Sophia was appalled that Felix would leave an officer outside on the steps. Sternly, Sophia asked, "Just why are we leaving an officer on the steps in a middle of deluge?"

"Pray forgive me milady, but the said officer is in a state of disarray," Felix answered with his plain and blunt voice, showing zero emotion on his expressionless face. Sophia wanted to wave a hand in front of his face to see if he flinched.

"Very well then. Please open the door and let us discover what this intrusion is all about." Sophia raised her arm toward the door, directing Felix to open it. Not knowing who was on the other side of the door or the purpose for the disturbance so late at night sent Sophia's heart racing. Her legs grew weak.

Could it possibly be? Perhaps the Home Office had everything wrong. Could Miles still be alive? Was he the officer on the other side of the door? Sophia dared to hope. With her fist to her heart, Sophia held her breath as Felix opened the door.

Was it Miles at the door? Find out by reading *The Loyal Officer*. Coming soon.

Sign-up to be notified of the release date for *The Loyal Officer* at www.marieleick.com.

Made in the USA
Columbia, SC
29 September 2023

23610089R00096